Boone cried out as his small body dropped low. "The mud is getting me!"

Lucy ran around the far edge of the sinkhole as Noah neared the boy. Sweat poured down his brow.

"Boone, I'm going to grab you. Jump toward me."

A shuddering groan sounded from the hole. No time. Noah leaped at Boone, lifting the child into his arms, then landing so he could launch up. His leap fell short as the massive tree rose and groaned out a hundred years of life coming to an end. The motion lifted Noah, slamming him backward into the trunk.

Noah shouted as they careened sideways. The root system was loose! He shouted Lucy's name as the ground gaped wide, forcing him and the child sideways. Cold wet dirt covered his arms and legs as they fell down, down into darkness and swallowed into the bowels of the earth.

Lucy's earsplitting scream was drowned out by the earth piling around him and Boone...

Kerry Johnson has been conversing with fictional characters and devouring books since her childhood in the Connecticut woods. A longtime member of ACFW, she's a seven-time Genesis Contest finalist and two-time winner. Kerry lives on the sunny, stormy west coast of Florida with her engineer husband, two teenage sons, eight-year-old niece and way too many books. She loves long walks, all creatures great and small, and iced chai tea.

Books by Kerry Johnson

Love Inspired Suspense

Snowstorm Sabotage
Tunnel Creek Ambush
Christmas Forest Ambush

Visit the Author Profile page at LoveInspired.com.

CHRISTMAS FOREST AMBUSH

KERRY JOHNSON

LOVE INSPIRED SUSPENSE

INSPIRATIONAL ROMANCE

LOVE INSPIRED® SUSPENSE
INSPIRATIONAL ROMANCE

Recycling programs
for this product may
not exist in your area.

ISBN-13: 978-1-335-51020-4

Christmas Forest Ambush

Love Inspired
22 Adelaide St. West, 41st Floor
Toronto, Ontario M5H 4E3, Canada
www.LoveInspired.com

Printed in U.S.A.

From the end of the earth will I cry unto thee,
when my heart is overwhelmed:
lead me to the rock that is higher than I.
For thou hast been a shelter for me,
and a strong tower from the enemy.
—*Psalm* 61:2-3

For my mom.
Your faith, prayers and especially your love have
shown me God's grace all the days of my life. I love you.

ONE

Lucy Taylor hated driving through the forest at night.

Scratch that.

She hated driving *alone* through stormy Sumter National Forest at night.

Technically it wasn't storming anymore. Lucy glanced in the rearview mirror at the back seat of her CR-V. And she wasn't really alone. Five-year-old Boone Harrington stared back.

"Are we there yet?"

Boone asked the age-old question many other foster children had asked while in her care. "Seven point five miles left, kiddo."

"What?"

"We'll be there soon."

Not soon enough.

Her apartment complex sat on the opposite end of Tunnel Creek. During the day, the thirty-minute drive from the county courthouse to her apartment on the outskirts of town through Sumter National Forest was doable, but at night, after the rain? Shadows, puddles and hairpin bends marked the way. A wild animal could emerge at any moment from the trees, and the moonlight barely reached the forest floor. Not to mention the troublesome memories of her childhood camping trip gone wrong.

Slow down. She eased up on the gas, squinting through the darkness to the next curve in the road.

Boone sniffled, the sad sound bringing to mind their meeting earlier. The tense faces of the judge and her supervisor, Melissa. The extra security. The heartbreaking details of what Boone's family had endured two days ago.

Home invasion. One parent dead. The other in a coma. A murderer still on the loose. And Boone, asleep in a pillow fort in his second-floor bedroom. Totally unaware.

All of it happening only three weeks before Christmas.

She curled her fingers over the steering wheel until the frayed rubber dug into her palms. Who would do this to the Harrington family?

"How much longer?" Boone asked.

"We're closer now than we were a minute ago." If only she could push a button and get there faster. "My high-density molecular transporter is broken, so we have to use this slow car."

"That's not really real."

She grinned at his frank perceptiveness, if not his lack of humor. Couldn't blame the poor boy if he never smiled again. Hopefully the shiny red remote control car she'd wrapped for a surprise early Christmas present would lift his spirits in the meantime.

Tonight he'd sleep in the second bedroom at her apartment while they waited on the judge's decision for Boone's temporary guardianship. Most likely he'd go to his maternal aunt and uncle in Greenville. The ruling could take a day or two, and her supervisor, Melissa, would mediate for now. In the meantime, Boone Harrington was her responsibility.

Unease trickled down her spine like ice water.

As a caseworker for the State of South Carolina, she was accustomed to caring for at-risk kids. Three days here, a week there. Sometimes just an overnighter. But this situation was different. It was drenched in the blood of Boone's family members. His dad, District Attorney Ryan Harrington, was dead, and Boone's mom lay in a medically induced coma until the swelling on her brain subsided. *If* it subsided.

Lucy's shoulders drooped as she pictured Boone's mom in the ICU at Tunnel Creek Hospital.

Though the hospital report stated the child was fine physically, Boone was no doubt traumatized. Sleep-deprived. Scared. Worried for his mom. And she didn't blame him one bit.

She considered her brief conversation with a Greenville detective before leaving the courthouse. He recommended an officer tail her on the way home, but the one assigned to her had been called away to a traffic incident. Her stomach flip-flopped. Having company on the pitch-black road might've alleviated this attack of nerves.

Wintry air slipped into the vehicle, sending chills across her skin. She adjusted the car's heater and peered through the windshield. At least the rain had stopped. The moon hung low in the sky, and half-dressed trees cast eerie shadows across the road, like tall skinny people with multiple arms reaching out for her...

Stop it, Lucy. She'd driven this road through Sumter National Forest dozens of times after court. During home visits in Tunnel Creek and nearby towns. While she much preferred city streets to closed-in country roads, she knew this route fairly well.

Everything will be fine.

A flicker of light behind them halted her internal pep talk. Her gaze glued to the rearview mirror. A vehicle appeared. Had the police officer been freed up to follow her after all?

The headlights brightened as the vehicle approached. It looked like a truck because it sat higher up than her SUV, with no sign of police lights or a siren. Why were they driving so fast? Lucy strangled the steering wheel. She was on one of the windiest sections of Forest Parkway, and the dividing line was solid for a long while. Trees hugged the roadside, leaving little room for impatient drivers to pass.

She drew in a slow breath and squared her shoulders. "You'll have to wait, buddy."

"What?" Boone piped up. "Who's Buddy?"

"I'm talking to another driver." She hesitated. "Why don't you close your eyes and rest?"

"What if it's the bad man?"

Invisible hands settled around her windpipe. "The bad man is far away. It's probably—"

The truck surged forward, ramming the right side of her bumper. Her words tore from her throat as her SUV veered across the line. She tapped the brakes and struggled to right their course, her pulse rising faster than the speedometer dial. *Don't jerk the wheel, don't jerk—*

A second smash to the bumper sent them reeling to the other shoulder. Boone wailed. Her purse dumped on the floorboard at the sudden change of direction, and she slammed the brakes to keep from sideswiping the trees. Branches scratched the doors as she steered onto the road again and rammed her foot on the gas pedal.

They pulled away from the truck. *Not fast enough.* Boone shouted, but the pounding in her ears eclipsed every other sound. Their pursuer zoomed in. Her heart thrashed against her ribs as the truck rode her bumper, swerving back and forth like the driver was inebriated. But instinct told her the person was doing exactly what they meant to do.

Harm them. Or worse…

"Hang on!" She floored the gas as they crested a small rise at a dangerous speed. Her stomach shot into her throat and Boone yelped in the back seat. The CR-V landed hard, metal crunching underneath. She gaped at the rearview mirror, her chest heaving. The truck flew over the hill, too, not far behind. Lucy moaned as the headlights closed in, blinding her.

Another smash sent her onto the narrow shoulder again. Her tires slid across the muddy ground, branches scraping the windows. She fought the SUV back onto the road. The *clack* of her cell phone tumbling off the console and hitting the rubber floor mats near the pedals drenched her skin in ice.

She needed to call 9-1-1. How long would it take authorities to get to them in the middle of the forest? What if—

What if the police didn't make it in time?

She couldn't risk searching for her cell at the moment, and she needed to calm her breathing or she'd black out. Focus on driving. For Boone. The truck had fallen back, but the vehicle's brights still invaded her SUV, keeping the driver's identity a mystery.

"Miss Lucy, go faster, faster!"

I'm trying to go faster, she thought. Her leg muscles burned as the speedometer crept up. Sixty-five. Sixty-eight. Seventy-one. She panted, concentrating on the dark, winding road. They drove at double the speed limit now.

Her Honda's engine revved, but it couldn't outrun the truck. Headlights flooded the interior of her car as the unrelenting vehicle closed in. "Hold on!"

The next impact knocked her body forward. The seat belt caught her, but she lost her grip on the wheel. The car spun, the forest rushing toward them. Branches snapped and glass cracked. She screamed as they crashed into the woods, the momentum pushing them through a wooden fence.

Boone's cries filled her ears as her SUV slid downward. Past trees, out into the open. Suddenly the truck headlights were gone. Where were they? Where had the trees gone, and their pursuer? Her car skated through a small clearing. She regained a hold of the steering wheel but the SUV twisted and turned out of her control.

Mud. They were sliding downhill on mud.

Wait—were they near Broken Branch Ridge?

Darkness bled through the windows, giving nothing away as her car oozed downward, the mud gripping her tires. Steering was useless. Where was the truck?

"Ms. Lucy!"

"I'm here. Try to stay still."

The sliding sensation slowed as a metallic crunching came from under the SUV's frame. Had the mud carried them over rocks? The car bumped something, then stopped. They teetered back and forth on the edge…of what? A rock? A lookout.

Were they at Broken Branch Ridge? Local teenagers dared each other to climb the side of the steep ridge during summer. It'd seemed reckless to her then, and now? Now it meant a sheer drop of thirty feet or so—right into the river.

Her mind spun. How deep was the water?

"Please, God." Her simple childhood faith was reawakened, tender and bruised from the hard edges of life and weakened by its bitterness. "We need You to save us."

The car creaked and groaned for several seconds as though trying to balance itself. Was this it, then? Stopped on the edge of a cliff? Her heart swooped like a frightened bird behind her ribs. All around was darkness. She wiggled, testing her arms and legs. Would the doors open?

Could she risk trying at this point?

The car creaked and groaned, then dipped sideways. Lucy gasped. It felt like a horrific dream. Her stomach lifted into her throat, and her inhalation turned into a scream that got caught up in the *whoosh* of fast-moving air.

They were falling.

Ranger Noah Holt pulled off his light-weight rain parka, shaking the water droplets away. He folded the jacket adorned with the Forest Ranger emblem and placed it back inside his pack. Then he retrieved a stick of jerky, gnawing off a hunk of it with a grimace. The snack tasted about as close to cardboard as food could get, but the rations weren't meant to taste good. They were supposed to raise his energy level, which was currently flatlining.

He pulled up his sleeve to check the time, then remembered his Timex Expedition was at home in need of a battery change. He'd already hiked seven and a half miles through the northwestern portion of Sumter National Forest repainting yellow trail marker blazes not easily accessible by road. Noah had one more trail blaze to paint before returning to the Whisper Mountain Tunnel ranger station. Then he'd head home for a three-week vacation.

He lifted his thermos from a side pocket, chasing down another mouthful of dry meat. The moon hid behind the leftover storm clouds, and a nip in the air promised winter would arrive in full force soon. Maybe they'd even get snow out of this weather system.

White Christmases were rare in western South Carolina, but these early December temps had been so low that a snowy Christmas might just happen.

He gazed up at the stars. When was the last time he had three whole weeks off over Christmas and New Year's? He couldn't remember. But he wouldn't be sitting on his duff. Instead, he was heading several hours north to hike a section of the AT in Virginia. From Cove Mountain to Rockfish Gap. One hundred and nine miles. Snow or not, conquering the entire Appalachian Trail was a bucket list item he was determined to finish by the time he turned thirty-five. Six more years. Slowly but surely, section by section, he'd do it.

Still, the idea of that much time off was unsettling. His supervisor, Derek, had pressed the issue, saying Noah hadn't been himself lately and needed time away.

It's the holidays, Derek had teased. *Do something inside for once. Watch a Christmas movie, man. Meet a girl.*

Meet a girl. Right. Not after...

Tessa's face and bright blue eyes came to mind, but he pushed them away.

Noah took another bite, grinding the jerky to a pulp in his cheek. Working—spending time in God's creation—was enjoyable for him. Especially around the holidays, when bittersweet childhood memories taunted him. His parents. The way they'd cared for each other. The way Christmas had always meant family time. Singing. Mom baking cookies. Presents despite not having a lot of material things. The Christmas concert Mom organized at the orphanage in Cameroon, where his parents had served as missionaries until his dad's untimely death.

After that, everything changed.

He released a sigh loaded with memories he didn't want to remember.

Maybe Derek was right.

Though he loved his job at Sumter, some days the satisfaction of catching poachers, locating a lost hiker or protecting an endangered animal rang hollow. He wasn't sure why, since being outside still gave him a thrill and left him feeling fulfilled. He knew his work was part of God's purpose for him. *Help others while maintaining God's creation.*

Admittedly it'd been tough to shake the dull emptiness plaguing him after losing his friend, fellow ranger Willard Tuttle, last year. Another reason to lose himself on the AT for a few days. The older man had been shot after stumbling upon a gun trafficking ring's hiding spot in Sumter. Both Noah and his brother, Jasper, a police officer who'd almost been killed alongside

Willard, had dealt with guilt over Willard's death.

It didn't help that Jasper was newly married to his high school girlfriend, Kinsley Miller. Noah had never seen Jasper so happy—so content—and at times Noah fought off feelings of envy at the genuine affection Jasper and Kinsley shared.

He stepped on a dry twig, relishing the crunch of the dead wood under his boot. Romance meant complications. Ultimatums. Certain losses of freedom that Noah wasn't ready to give up. Especially in his line of work, when extended time outside was often required. An image of Tessa's face appeared again.

An unnatural metallic sound resonated through the forest. Noah froze, whipped his head around.

He listened, trying to pinpoint the location. An 18-wheeler on the parkway, downshifting? Possible, though the big rigs rarely drove these roads. Hikers? Better not be. The wilderness portion of the forest had signs warning visitors that after-hours activities were off-limits this time of year. Hunting season and colder weather precluded the busy campsites of spring, summer and early fall. Not to mention, camping was only allowed in certain sections of the forest, and this rugged, rocky area around Broken Branch River and Dogwood Falls wasn't one of them.

Better check it out. He shoved his thermos back in the side pocket of his pack and took off at a fast clip down the trail.

A shockingly heavy splash flipped his thoughts from steady to stunned.

He ground his jaw. Had someone thrown trash off the ridge, thinking it would be carried downriver? Better not be dumpers. He'd about lost it on the last ones he'd detained and fined.

Something else Derek had mentioned while trying to convince Noah to take time off.

Another high-pitched noise scalded the air. Noah froze midstride. Was that a woman's scream? Couldn't be. Probably just two raccoons fighting over a crayfish at the river's edge.

He set off toward the sound. Water levels were elevated throughout the county, and Broken Branch was bank-full. The river's white-capped, splashing song usually calmed him, but tonight something felt off. Broken Branch Ridge glinted under the moonlight, a haggard rock wall that teens and adrenaline junkies climbed up and jumped off.

At the bottom, a small SUV bobbed like a child's bathtub toy on the water's surface.

"No way." *A car. In the river. How...?*

No time to figure out the *hows*. He had to get out there. What was the fastest way across? *Willard's bridge.* He cut left through the underbrush, toward the bridge used by hikers to cross.

Another cry carried over, this one from a child. A sudden chill spread through his limbs.

"God, please get me over there in time." His anger and regret about Willard's death had created a divide between him and the Lord, but this situation—this called for heavenly backup.

He tugged out his CB radio.

"Red Knight, come in. Red Knight, do you copy? Brown Tree, over."

Static crackled for a moment, then the line cleared.

"Brown Tree, where are…" Derek's voice was too garbled to understand.

Noah growled under his breath. He must be in a bad reception pocket. "Red Knight. Call 9-1-1. Car in Broken Branch River. Send help by air. Over."

Unbroken static was the only answer. No telling if Derek had heard or understood what he said. Noah jogged hard to the riverbank. Ferns crunched underfoot as he headed several yards downriver, then mounted the steps of the bridge. In its former life, it was a huge old oak, but now it lay split in half, a simple wood railing rising three feet on both sides. Algae and lichen claimed large spots on its length because the canopy of trees didn't allow much sunlight in. Hence the warning signs at both ends of the bridge about its slippery surface.

He peered at the swirling Broken Branch below. The unrelenting current drowned summer's leftover weeds along its banks. The diving pool, where the car had fallen, was over twenty feet in depth at this point.

Good thing, too. Otherwise…

He shook his head and started across, palm skimming the railing. His boots gripped the slick surface if he kept his steps precise. Slow. What wasn't slow were the questions racing through his mind. How had the vehicle slid the thirty or forty yards to the edge of the ridge? Wasn't there a guardrail along that portion of the parkway? A fence at least? How many people were inside?

The child cried out again. *God, help me.* Noah patted the two-way radio set in its holder on his side. He needed to reach Derek again but first he had to get the people out, get them on solid ground.

He squinted upriver as the roaring waters released a blinding, hissing mist into the air.

Noah kept a hand on the railing and moved purposefully along the bridge's length, eyes pinned to the dark bobbing vehicle. His pulse thundered in his ears. Normally, natural debris plus canoes and kayaks fit neatly under the bridge, but today—with an actual car and water levels up—that wasn't happening. The car would smash into the man-made bridge. And Noah wasn't sure whether the vehicle or the aged old oak would win.

Dogwood Falls lay two hundred yards downriver. He had to get them out *now*.

Noah yanked off his pack, pulling out his rescue rope. Hooking it on his belt and then around the bridge railing, he flicked his flashlight headgear on, then faced the SUV.

From what he could see, a female sat in the front seat, airbags deployed around her. Her movements were frantic, her body twisting around like she was tugging at something in the back seat. *The child he'd heard.* Noah's hands tightened on the rope, his shoulders rigid and leg muscles locked.

Thirty feet.

Twenty feet.

He and the woman made eye contact in the amber moonlight, and his chest constricted.

The car floated closer, sinking deeper until the headlights were submerged. Just then, the woman's head pushed through the window, a mass of long dark hair covering part of her face.

"Help! Please, get him!"

"Is he unbuckled?" Noah shouted, gesturing with his arms. Could the woman see him in the dark, or did his headlight blind her? He clicked the light dimmer.

The car lurched to his right, rotating to hit the bridge on the driver's side. The impact came instantly, and the oak bridge trembled in response. A crack echoed over the rushing waters. Was that the bridge or the car?

Suddenly a child's head appeared through

the driver's side window. Noah bent forward, reaching. A boy with shaggy brown hair and a small frame. Noah looped the rope around the child's waist and lifted him high and away from the turbulent waters and unsteady vehicle.

"I've got you." The child clung to Noah, reminding him of his nephew, Gabriel. "Come on!" He motioned at the woman. One down, one to go.

She scrambled through the window, pushing off the seat before diving to wrap her arms around the closest section of the railing. The current crashed into her, and she slipped into the water. *No.* Her terrified cry shot into the air just before her head went under. Noah sat and kicked out a leg, pressing his boot to the hood of the vehicle, fighting to keep himself and the boy safely on the bridge while stopping her from being crushed between the car and the wood.

"Grab that!" he shouted when her head broke the surface. He pointed to a huge branch caught under the bridge, then quickly disentangled the rope from the child.

She threw out her arms and latched on to the branch, her features a mask of determination.

"Now grab the rope!" He tossed it her way, but water splashed in her face as she reached for it. She lost her grip on the branch, and the current carried her farther to Noah's left. Foaming white water encircled her head as she bobbed toward an eddy that whirlpooled under the bridge. He hauled the rope back and readied to toss it again.

She swam for a smaller branch sticking off the bridge. Barely a foot in length, it wouldn't hold her for long. Still, she stuck to it like lichen on bark.

"Miss Lucy!" The child yanked Noah's arm, like he wanted him to dive in and save her. Having the boy so close risked both of them falling in.

Noah hefted him in a side hold, then dashed to the steps, setting the child on the top one. "Stay right here," he warned.

He scrambled back out to the middle section, his headlight beam examining the churning water. The woman's eyes sought his in the dark. His relief that she was still holding on was short-lived as the current spun her around and farther to the other side.

"Grab this," he shouted over the thundering river, then tossed the rope. She grasped it with one hand then both. *Thank the Lord.*

"I'm going to pull you in. Hang on."

He tugged her closer, pulling slowly so she had a chance to haul herself over the edge, between the railing, and catch her breath. She used one hand to grab the railing while the other arm fell over the bridge. Long dark hair hung over her back and clothes—some kind of fancy clothes. *City person.* She climbed up, huddling on the tree bridge.

The boy had called her Lucy, so his guess was she wasn't the child's mom. Maybe an aunt, taking her nephew out for a movie.

"It's okay. I've got you." He set a hand on her trembling shoulder, then glanced back to make sure the boy was still in the same spot. They needed to get off the bridge and onto dry land. The tree was probably damaged, plus temps would dip into the upper thirties tonight. Dangerously low for someone in soaking clothes. "Let's get off this bridge and get you two warmed up. Then I'll radio this in."

The woman turned, and Noah had to remind himself to breathe. She looked about his age, near thirty, he'd guess. Oval-shaped brown eyes met his, set under dark arched brows. They were red-rimmed under the headlight's glare, and fear drew her mouth into a tight line.

"Please. Wait. I need to tell you what happened…"

It was hard to hear her over the river, plus she seemed to be struggling to get words out. Had she hit her head in the accident?

"It's okay. I'm a forest ranger, ma'am." He gestured at the vehicle, which now seemed to be caught on something below the surface. "I need to contact my supervisor. Call in authorities. File a report. Get you both to the hospital."

"No, it's not…" She closed her eyes and tucked her chin. Was she crying? Or just in shock?

"Ma'am?" Wait a minute—had she committed a crime? He blinked hard. "Is this an abducted child?"

Her head flew up, eyes flashing. "N-no. Please. Listen. S-someone just ran us off the road."

"Are you saying this was done on purpose?"

"I think so." Her breaths released in continuous clouds between them.

He lowered his voice. "Domestic dispute?"

"What? No."

She shook her head, then glanced at the little boy on the steps on the side of the bridge. "No. I'm his caseworker. I work for the foster care system. The state? I'm pretty sure this isn't about me." She nudged her chin at the child, not saying anything but her motions making it clear.

Someone was after the boy? Noah drew his head back. "Why him?"

She flicked a piece of wet hair from her cheek, then addressed the child. "Boone, are you okay?"

"I'm cold. And I don't wanna ever, ever do that again."

"Me, either. Let's get you warmed up." She rose on wobbly legs, staring at Noah for a long moment. He held her gaze, frowning. What was this about?

The woman edged past him on the bridge, sinking down to wrap her arms around the child's—Boone's—shoulders. The uncommon name sparked a memory. A recent, awful memory.

Boone Harrington? The son of the murdered district attorney. Noah gave her a cursory nod as his mind hurtled toward this startling new reality.

She'd stated that someone had run them off the road, and he had no reason to doubt her story. The evidence was right before his eyes. Which meant the district attorney's on-the-run murderer was after his young son...and the child's caseworker.

Noah thrust his hand through his hair. Water droplets sprayed his face, stung his eyes. After eight years as a forest ranger, he'd seen his share of odd circumstances. Unexpected situations and helpless people. The vastness of the woods humbled even the most experienced outdoorsman and woman. But this topped them all. Because it appeared that he and this woman were now tangled up in the biggest murder case in the state.

TWO

Lucy tried not to stare at the man. If he hadn't identified himself as a forest ranger, his green uniform and formidable backpack would've given it away. He was tall, at least a head taller than she, which was rare. Not to mention the blinding headlight on his forehead that made him look like some creature-of-the-night cyclops. He'd dimmed it during their conversation at least. When his mouth turned down with understanding about who Boone was, relief had flooded her chest. The ranger seemed to grasp the importance of not speaking everything aloud in front of the child. Boone was terrified, wet and freezing, and she wouldn't add to that by recounting all he'd been through.

An ear-piercing *creak* came from the center of the bridge, where their rescuer still stood. The wood shifted beneath him. Her hand shot out to steady herself and Boone. Was the bridge breaking?

He flashed the headlight over the length of the wood. "We have to get off the bridge."

In one fluid motion, he darted over, lifted Boone like he was a bouquet of flowers, wrapped an arm around her and carried them down the stairs. Moving as one unit away from the bridge. The heel of one of her soaked ankle boots caught on a tree root, but his grip and strength kept her from pitching forward.

The unyielding sound of cracking wood chased them farther up a small incline. Away from the river. Her heart skipped a beat as what had happened replayed in her mind. Had Ryan Harrington's murderer done this? But Boone was a *child*. He hadn't witnessed any of the crime. And it was almost Christmas. Her stomach twisted. If only another police officer had followed them home, this wouldn't have happened.

Sharp brambles nipped her shins through her slacks, and the muddy ground slurped at her ankle boots. Several feet above the riverbank, they burst onto a narrow, well-worn trail. The ranger slowed, and Lucy's legs gave out. She tumbled onto a mossy boulder and covered her face with her hands.

"Ma'am, are you injured?"

"No. Yes." She blew out a hard breath, swiping at her cheeks. Fighting back the feeling of the forest closing in on her. "I'm not really sure at this point. I... I can't believe what just happened."

"I've never seen anything like this before. You're probably still in shock."

No doubt about that. And now she and Boone were stuck in the worst place possible—the woods. At night. She clenched her teeth and worked to bring her inhaling and exhaling into a slower rhythm.

The ranger placed Boone beside her, then reached back and tugged a blanket from his backpack. Set it around them. It was surprisingly warm for being so light.

"Thank you."

"If you're not hurt, we need to keep moving."

"Please, give us a minute to rest." She shivered.

He set his pack down then retrieved a black object from his hip. A radio? He turned the knob, and the loud, crackling static made her flinch.

"Red Knight? Red Knight, come in. This is Brown Tree. Repeat, this is Brown Tree. Car in Broken Branch River, do you copy?"

The only answer was more static. He tried again, then a third time. Finally, he clicked it off and set it back on his hip. "We must be in a dead pocket."

"Who is Red Knight?"

"My supervisor, Derek." The ranger scrutinized Boone, then looked back at her. "It's imperative to get you both to a warm place. Some type of shelter. Hypothermia can set in even with the temps above freezing."

A whistling *ping-ping* cut through the air near them. What was that? Another *ping* followed, thumping into a tree trunk two feet past the ranger. He gave a shout, then dove to the ground, bringing her and Boone along. Pain cut down her left arm as Boone's knee rammed it.

"Stay still." The ranger turned his headlight off, holding them in an awkward embrace against the ground. His pack lay near their heads. Only his elbows kept them from being squished beneath him. Boone whimpered.

"It's okay, little man," the ranger soothed in a strained voice. "We're just playing a game of hide-and-seek."

"I never played outside at nighttime before."

"This is professional level hide-and-seek. Shh."

She lifted her head slightly. "Was that—"

"Yes," he cut her off. "From up on the ridge."

She rested her forehead on a soggy stick. Someone was shooting at them from the ridge, which meant the person who'd rammed her vehicle was still pursuing them…straight into the forest. A violent tremor worked over her body.

Her fingers sank into the soggy earth. Pebbles and twigs pressed her palms as cold dirt crammed under her nails. Whoever was after Boone was determined to follow through. But why? Her throat thickened. He was a sweet, innocent child. Not a threat to anyone. "What do we do?"

"Stay still for now. I'll keep trying my radio. Otherwise, we're on our own out here."

"There's no cell service?"

"We're in a national forest. Some areas have reception, some don't."

"So even if I had my cell, it wouldn't help."

"Right. The weather can cause problems, too. There's a large storm system moving through the area the next twenty-four hours. And we're pretty remote right now. We must be in a dead zone."

That wasn't encouraging. "Do you carry a cell phone?"

"Yes, but I rarely use it. Dead zone," he repeated, as though she wanted to hear that term again. The irony of being shot at and being stuck in a dead zone in the woods was a little much.

"Should we try to get farther away from the ridge?"

"Not yet." He adjusted his elbows to give them more room.

"But what if the person up *there* comes down *here*?"

"Our chances are better hiding here and waiting until he gives up than becoming moving targets."

"True, but—"

"Please. You'll have to trust me."

Trust him. She rolled a twig between her fingers. She met him ten minutes ago. But he had saved them from her car on the river. Protected them when the bridge cracked and now, when shots were fired.

He cleared this throat. "What happened up there? Just…basics."

"We were driving to my apartment near Tunnel Creek Elementary. I had just come from the courthouse. We were figuring out temporary custody and meeting with the judge."

"Right. Everything is still…ongoing, I assume?" he asked. "No arrests yet?"

"Yes. And no." She cupped Boone's little hands to warm them up, careful to keep the conversation as general as possible. "Halfway home, a truck appeared. It sped up like he was going to pass, but the person stayed close behind me for maybe a quarter of a mile. I'm not sure. Then he rammed the bumper." She shuddered. "Two or three times."

"He tailed you, then. Knew you were going that way. Did you get a look at the vehicle?"

"Just that it was a truck. Dark blue or brown? I'm not sure. I was so focused on trying to stay on the road."

"I understand." They waited a few more

minutes, the rushing river keeping her nerves on edge. Lucy patted Boone's arm and tried to ignore the strange noises coming from the forest. Snapping, whistling wind. An animal—an owl?—hooting. She winced. Being here reminded her of why she disliked the woods. Reminded her of the family camping trip that ended badly when she was ten, and how it had changed her life forever.

The ranger rolled his large frame to the left, then unzipped his bag. After retrieving a bulky pair of binoculars, he slowly flipped over, setting the gadget to his face.

Several beats of silence followed. Lucy sat up. "Anyone up there?"

"It doesn't appear so. Stay down."

She ducked back down. "You can see in the dark with those?"

"Yes."

She waited for him to elaborate. "So that's good, they're gone, right?"

"Not necessarily. The person might've moved to a closer location."

She eyed the bushes and trees along the trail. Where would they go?

"We need to get away from the river. I can't hear anything or anyone approaching us with the water's noise." He squinted up at the night sky. "And the temperature is dropping. There's a weather system coming through that will make being outside dangerous."

Which meant cold. But where would they find shelter? Boone curled into himself, shivering. She reached over to rub his back. Her heart twinged at the tiny bumps of his spine against her hand. "What an adventure we're having tonight."

"I don't wanna adventure."

She smiled at his candor. "Me, either."

"My chest hurts."

She felt around him on the ground. "Are you laying on a rock?"

"No, my air hurts."

His air? *Oh, no.* His asthma. His bag still sat in her car, with his emergency inhaler and a few handpicked toys from his room that the first caseworker on scene had chosen. Lucy's pulse throbbed in her temples. What if he needed his inhaler?

"What is it?" The ranger gave her a measured look.

"There's something in my car he needs." Pushing oxygen through her own lungs suddenly became harder. What if his medicine ended up submerged? Those inhalers weren't waterproof.

"It's too dangerous right now, ma'am."

"Since we're stuck here together, maybe we should be on a first-name basis? My name is Lucy. And yours is…?"

"Noah."

He was definitely a man of few words. "I'm sorry, but we'll have to go back and get Boone's bag." And maybe her purse. But the medication was of utmost importance. She glanced at Boone. Showing the child how upset she was about not having the inhaler might cause more problems. She willed her voice lower and calmer. "Please."

"You know what just happened." He emphasized each word. "It's not safe."

Neither was the boy suffering an asthma attack. She caught the ranger's eye, then pretended she was using an inhaler, dragging in a heavy breath to show him what she meant.

Understanding dawned in his face. "Ten-four." The ranger—Noah—turned away, rummaging through his pack on the ground. "I carry an epinephrine pen."

She twisted the edge of her damp blouse. Giving Boone an injection similar to a shot versus two simple puffs of the inhaler wasn't ideal. Then again, neither was getting struck by a bullet.

Still, handing over lifesaving care of this child to a man she barely knew unsettled her. "You said you're a ranger?"

"I am. With the US Forest Service."

She waited for more details, but he volunteered nothing else. "Do you have a last name?"

"It's Holt."

Noah Holt?

"Any chance you're related to Brielle Holt?" Lucy had moved to Tunnel Creek from Greenville her junior year, and Bri had been one of the few friendly faces at Tunnel Creek High.

"Bri's my younger sister."

Her spine loosened. He wasn't a complete stranger, then. "How is she doing?"

"Better than we currently are." He wiped leaves off his shirt. "She runs her own antique business a few miles outside Tunnel Creek."

"That's great. Bri was one of the nicest people at TCH. She always said hi to me." Lucy paused. "She made a difficult time in my life easier."

"I'm glad she was there for you." He snorted softly. "Sure would be nice if she took the time to say hi to her family, too."

What did he mean? "She's probably really busy with her own store."

"That she is." He swept the area with his binoculars before placing them back into his bag. "Time to move. We have to get to the bottom of the falls. Reception usually picks up down there."

"Wait—what about his inhaler?"

"The car is most likely submerged at this point. Otherwise, I would go back. And I'm not sure the location of the…" He grimaced, then waved finger guns at her. "Let's get away from the river. I'll radio this in and call for medics. We should be out of here in one to two hours."

Her heart stuttered. "It takes that long for help to arrive?"

"It will out here." He rose to his feet, his movements fast and sure as he settled Boone in his arms. "Move quickly and quietly." He pulled a jacket out of his bag and handed it to her. "Here. Put this on."

"Thank you." Lucy stood, slipping on the oversized coat, then wrapped the blanket around Boone like a poncho. She noticed Noah turned so his back was facing the ridge as he moved. Protecting Boone? Warmth spread across her middle. Maybe Grumpy Ranger wasn't so bad.

And he was right. They had to find shelter and get both of them dry. But what happened if the little boy's asthma acted up? She hated to use an EpiPen. Adding trauma to more trauma. Her stomach quivered. *One thing at a time.* Boone's breathing seemed even and quiet, other than an occasional whimper. No wheezing or whistling that she could hear. Noah carrying him helped keep the child's activity to a minimum, too.

Would rescuers or EMTs be able to reach them? And what would happen if not and they were outside overnight, especially with it getting colder like Noah said? From what she remembered from her state certification classes, cold weather often bothered asthmatics. Her supervisor, Melissa, hadn't shared much about the child's condition due to the rushed circumstances, other than passing along the inhaler and a few of Boone's toys and clothes in the bag.

Noah set off, and Lucy hurried to keep up. They weaved through trees so quickly everything spun in her peripheral vision. Despite the darkness, he moved like a man with full sunlight on his back. He must know these woods inside and out.

A few minutes later, he slowed, met her eyes briefly. "There's rock up ahead. It'll be wet from the rain. Easy to slip. Stay close, watch your step."

"Ten-four," she repeated his earlier expression.

He blinked at her for a moment, then turned and resumed his breakneck pace.

Did he ever smile? She shook her head.

They headed down the trail, then cut across an eerily silent stretch of knee-high ferns. The nonstop *whoosh* of the river faded as they traveled farther from it. Shouldering his hefty bag and Boone, who had to weigh at least forty pounds, Noah seemed to move with ease. His strides were long and quick, while her chest was heaving by the time they came upon the area he'd warned her about.

The waterfall. Stair steps of granite covered the ground, and from what she could make out in the dark, the landscape sloped downhill sharply. The waterfall sounded like a dozen kitchen faucets left on full blast.

The ground steepened, and the rock increased, sticking out at odd angles. Slippery, too. He hadn't been kidding. This would've been tough in regular hiking boots during the daylight. Her cold, wet ankle boots with their one-inch heels were definitely not made for the uneven forest floor or wet rock.

By the time they reached the bottom, sweat dampened her brow despite the chilly air. Noah strode through another carpet of ferns toward the pool where the falls emptied. It wasn't a huge waterfall, but the spray still coated them with a cold sheen of mist.

"Congratulations." He pointed. "You just hiked Dogwood Falls."

Never again. "You've been here before?"

"Many times." He hesitated. "It's one of my favorite spots in this part of the forest."

She glanced at the top of the falls. The sensation of being watched sent a shiver down her arms, and she crossed them over her chest.

"Did you see something?" Noah asked.

"No. I'm just jumpy."

"Tell me immediately if you see some-one."

"I will."

He set off again, and she scurried after him. They followed a winding creek that split off the waterfall pool, leading them deeper into the woods. The moonlight dimmed as the forest closed in, creating a weighty sense of claustrophobia that pressed down on her shoulders. She focused on Noah, who continually skimmed the area with his gaze.

She stayed as close beside him as she could without making it awkward. "Do you think the person on the ridge could cross the bridge now? Since the wood was breaking?"

"Hard to say."

That wasn't much of an answer. "So, no one can cross the bridge?"

"If the river splits the wood apart, then no. But there are two narrow sections up-stream where the riverbanks are less than ten feet apart. Those are shallower sections. And there's another bridge one-third of a mile upriver."

Well, that wasn't good news.

"I'm sorry the bridge is damaged."

He adjusted his hold on Boone. The boy clung to him like a bear cub to its mother. "It's a bridge. It can be rebuilt."

She blinked at Noah. That was certainly true. "I'm glad you were nearby. I don't think we could have…" she let her voice fade …*made it out alive otherwise.*

He turned to meet her eyes. "Is someone waiting for you at your apartment? A husband or roommate?"

"No. Only my fish, Bubbles. He's a betta." Could she sound more pitiful? Wait—was that a hint of a *smile* on his face, or was the moonlight playing tricks on her? "Why?"

"Normally, a significant other would notify authorities when you don't arrive at your apartment or answer your phone. If there's no relative or friend living with you, it may take longer for authorities to find out you're both missing."

"Sometimes I drive to Greenville on weekends to visit my brother." She shrugged. "I might even be moving there soon, if I get the promotion I'm hoping for."

"Neighbors may assume that's where you are when you don't arrive home tonight or tomorrow."

She grimaced. Which meant, unless his radio worked, they were stranded out here.

They slowed, and Noah situated them beneath a massive tree. He set Boone down at the base, then stretched his back and rolled his head side to side. Perspiration shone on his forehead, the only indication he was exerting himself. How many hours had he been out here today? All day?

She tied her damp hair into a knot, then sank down and wrapped an arm around Boone's shoulders. "Are you warm enough?"

"Yeah. Can I sleep in my bed tonight?"

"I'm sorry, I don't think so. It looks like

we get to camp out here in the woods tonight." She squelched the tremor that took over her muscles. *Unfortunately.*

Boone yawned. How small and defenseless he felt against her. How could someone go after a sweet child like this? The child told authorities he hadn't seen any of the killers' faces. He'd been asleep in his room during the murder.

A thought struck like a blow.

Ryan Harrington had been under police protection before his murder. And she was pretty sure she'd read about a local police officer who'd been part of the Whisper Mountain gun trafficking ring.

She fought to keep her arm from shaking as she held the child. What if getting Boone to the police actually put him in more danger?

Noah pulled out his radio again. The click revealed more static. He repeated the same thing he said by the river a few minutes ago, but only static answered. After three tries, he let out a frustrated grunt and shoved the radio back in its holder.

"Is it always this difficult to contact your supervisor? Or anyone else, for that matter?"

"No. Must be the weather and our location."

Her mind turned over Boone's precarious physical situation. "I was thinking, what if turning him into the police leads to...to more of this?"

"The authorities will keep him safe."

"How can you be sure?" How to say this about Boone's dad without upsetting the boy? She searched for the correct term. "The *district attorney* was supposed to have police surveillance at his house." Ryan Harrington had a police escort, or at least that had been reported. "And yet..."

She cut off her words as Noah's gaze crashed into hers.

And yet... *Ryan Harrington was dead.*

Noah crossed his arms. "I understand your concern." He pointed his chin toward Boone. "But getting him into police protection is the safest course of action. When

I'm able, I also have to let my supervisor know your car is still in the river."

"I don't care about my car."

"I do." He dropped his arms. "It's a biohazard. Your safety is paramount, first and foremost. But I also have to consider the chance that gasoline could leak into the water and wreak havoc on the environment. As far as the police, I'll call my brother and fill him in."

"Why your brother?"

"Jasper is an officer with Tunnel Creek PD." He drew his cell from his pack. Most likely, it wouldn't have reception, either, but he had to try.

Noah pulled up the keypad and hit Derek's number. The call wouldn't go through—no bars. He threw his head back. "Come on."

"An officer was supposed to follow me home." Her words wavered. "But something else came up and he didn't. Don't you find that a little strange, given what happened to this family?"

"Law enforcement prioritizes calls." He

hadn't heard any local law enforcement emergencies this evening. "Another call must've been deemed more urgent."

Boone wiggled his legs, his knees slapping into each other. Lucy spoke to the child then stood up, moving toward Noah and dropping her voice to a whisper. "What if the man finds out where we are, then ambushes us as we come out of the forest?"

His spine stiffened. "I know this area well. I'll do my best to keep you both safe."

"I believe you will. You have so far." She backed away from him as though she realized she'd pushed too hard. "What about hiding in the forest, like in a cabin or something, then waiting until the man is caught?"

What did she think this was, a Harrison Ford movie? "The police won't know to look for you two or the men after you unless we notify them this happened."

"Men? You think there's more than—"

"I have to go potty." Boone popped up

between them, his eyes the size of dinner plates.

"Okay, let's find a spot." She corralled the bouncing child around Noah, and he was reminded that he was rarely around tall women. His mom wasn't short, but she was still a few inches shy of his six-two. Lucy stood tall enough that her forehead reached his chin when they were face-to-face.

Reality kicked in. It was dark. Windy. A man with a gun was out there. Lucy and Boone had no idea where they were in the woods.

"I'll take him. Stay right here, by the tree." Noah grasped Boone's hand. "We won't go far."

He led the wiggly boy a few yards away, into a thicket of overgrown bushes jammed between two towering trees. He tried to stay within a fifteen-yard radius since the social worker—Lucy—seemed very much out of her element. Which, if he was being fair, most people in the woods were. While he couldn't blame her agitation about their predicament, he could stand to have two minutes of silence to consider the right course of action. The forest's quiet landscape had always cleared his mind. Calmed him. Amplified his prayers.

And he definitely needed to pray about this situation.

He and Boone ended up in a clearing populated mostly with slash pine. He slowed. "How about here?" Noah motioned at a felled pine a few feet ahead of them. Bushes grew up under the tree, making it a natural fence.

"I dunno." The child coughed twice.

His mind replayed Lucy's words as he scouted out a more private spot. *An officer was supposed to follow me home. But something else came up and he didn't.*

She was right. It *was* odd that an officer hadn't tailed her home. Irresponsible, even. Something about the situation didn't sit right. How could Boone's circumstances be deemed not important enough for an officer to follow them? Ryan Harrington's murder was without a doubt linked to the illegal arms ring that had been uncovered at the Whisper Mountain Tunnel last year. Noah knew more than most about the gun smuggling investigation because his brother, Jasper, had been closely involved in bringing it down.

And Willard Tuttle's death had made it personal.

Boone squirmed beside him, then coughed again.

He leaned down, cupped the child's shoulders. "You okay?"

Boone murmured an *uh-huh*, but his wiggling was a clear sign time was running out.

Noah pointed to a clump of ferns growing beneath a massive sweet gum at the edge of the clearing. "Here. Stand beside those. I'll face the other way." He turned, rubbing a palm down his face as a wave of weariness knocked into him. Once they were turned in to authorities, he might need a couple days to crash before driving up to Waynesboro to start off his next leg of the AT.

Boone tapped his arm ten seconds later. "All done."

Noah directed him back toward Lucy and his pack. Questions clogged his mind like debris in the river. Why couldn't he get through on the radio? Where was Derek? His supervisor tended toward micromanaging Noah and the five other rangers in their jurisdiction. Even on his days off, Derek liked to be involved in decisions, often asking for updates on fires in the dry season, poachers, equipment maintenance issues and lost hikers.

Still, Noah couldn't stop considering Lucy's question about turning them in. Would it create more problems for Boone? That shooter hadn't been warning them. The person had been given a kill order. By whom? His thoughts trailed off to Tunnel Creek Officer Dean Hammond, who had been busted with dirty hands in the gun smuggling ring. So yeah, sometimes good men went bad for the love of money.

It wasn't like they had lots of options, anyway. He could either keep trying to call Derek, or they had to find somewhere safe to spend the night. The child's asthma wasn't to be taken lightly, and he only had one EpiPen.

Get them to a shelter. Take care of immediate needs. Food. Hydration.

And rest, so they were up for hiking back to the ranger station tomorrow.

"I'm tired." Boone coughed again, a faint wheezing following the words. "My air hurts."

Noah's thoughts jerked back to the present. He scooped Boone up, cradling the boy, and set off for their hiding spot. His muscles caught fire from the high-pitched sounds coming from Boone with every exhalation. "I got you, buddy."

The temperature had dropped more. Had to be in the low forties now. In his training, he'd learned asthmatics could be triggered by cold weather and allergies. There wasn't much plant life alive in the forest this time of year, so this must be related to the cold.

"Try to breathe in your nose, then out through your mouth. Slow and deep, okay?"

"I'm…trying. My air hurts." Boone wheezed.

Noah lengthened his stride as he rushed toward Lucy. To his pack. It appeared that they'd need the EpiPen sooner rather than later. *God, please keep this child's airways open.* The hair on the back of his neck lifted. *And keep the shooter away, too.*

THREE

Lucy held Boone's little hands between her own, rubbing briskly to warm them up. And to distract him and herself from the alarming high-pitched rattling sound coming from his chest as he breathed.

A couple feet away, Noah withdrew the EpiPen from his pack, peeling away the protective plastic wrap. He squinted at the pen, then let out an ominous noise.

She released Boone's hands. "What is it?"

"No. How is this possible?"

She jumped up, hurrying over to Noah. He stood beneath the large tree, his formidable shoulders ramrod straight. She snatched the pen from him, peering at it. *Oh, no.* Under the glare of his headlight, the date plainly stated the pen expired a year ago.

"What do we do?" Her heart sank.

"This can't be right. I check my first aid kit at the beginning of each month to make sure things are up-to-date. I just looked through it." Frustration radiated off Noah. "It doesn't make sense."

At the moment, very little did. She covered her mouth with her fingertips to keep from weeping. "What do we do?"

"Try to contact help." He whipped out his radio and clicked it on. She rubbed her arms as the constant static sound filled her ears. Over and over, he spoke to the small black gadget. Why wasn't anyone answering? Hadn't he said reception was better down here at the base of the falls?

He let out a growl, then tried his cell. She didn't need to ask what was happening because his tense movements told the story. He still couldn't get through.

"There has to be something else." Her entire body quaked. Could the paramedics fly in with a helicopter? "Where's the nearest ranger station?"

He shook his head. "Almost three miles. My truck is there. But it's a strenuous hike in the daytime."

Meaning it would be even harder at night, especially with them slowing him down.

Noah lifted his chin, his eagle gaze landing on Boone. "Wait a minute. We can still use this. The medicine should still help."

"How do you know? Are you sure it won't hurt him?"

"Its potency may be weaker because it's expired, but it shouldn't hurt him. We have to try." He took the pen back and swerved around her, dropping in front of Boone. "Hey, buddy, can you be brave for me? I want to help so your air doesn't hurt anymore."

Boone gave a pitiful nod, staring at the EpiPen. His chest labored with each inhalation. Noah held out the pen instead of trying to hide it.

"This has medicine that will help you breathe better," he explained. "May I use it?"

"Uh-huh."

A few minutes later, Boone lay across Lucy's lap like a large puppy, his breathing blessedly clear. His arms and legs wiggled like tiny earthquakes were erupting beneath his skin. While the medicine had been expired, Noah was right. There had been enough left to open up Boone's restricted airways.

For the second time in one night, Lucy silently prayed. *Thank You, God.* It was strange to talk to God after all these years of silence, but it also felt...right.

Noah paced in front of them, eyes glued to Boone. He'd used the pen carefully, then soothed the child as he held him, like a father would. The thought surprised her. Was Noah married? Did he have children?

She turned, focused on Boone instead. "He's so much better. The wheezing has completely stopped. Thank you. That was a good idea to try it."

"It's the adrenaline in the medicine." Noah dropped to one knee, squinting at the little boy. "Thank the Lord there was enough left to help."

She tried not to stare at him. Noah was a believer?

"It'll wear off soon, then he'll be exhausted."

"I know I am." She closed her eyes and set the back of her head to the rock she'd propped herself against. It was cold, but solid. "I feel like I could sleep twelve hours."

"About that…" He hesitated, and she opened her eyes, meeting his. "I'm sure you heard I can't reach anyone. There's a big front coming through. Sometimes the weather affects the radios. But this is the worst I've ever seen it."

"Are you out here by yourself most of the time?"

"I am." He shrugged one shoulder as if it wasn't a big deal. "Part of the job."

What was that like, being alone so much? Her job kept her interacting with people a lot, all hours of the day and even night. It could be tiring, but she was helping children who often didn't have anyone else, and that was fulfilling. Necessary. She rubbed Boone's back. It was enough.

"I've considered our options." He rammed a hand through his hair. "Before we go any farther, I'm heading back to your car."

"What?" It was the last thing she expected him to say. "Now?"

"I sent my brother a text, but I don't think it went through." Noah pointed his chin at Boone, who had nodded off despite their conversation. "I want to try to get his bag. The medicine." He glanced around the sheltered alcove beneath a large tree where they rested. "And you're well hidden here. I can move faster alone."

That was true. She'd sensed his impatience while they were descending the rocks to the base of the waterfall.

"It'll take me six minutes to the top of the falls, then a few more to the section of the Broken Branch where your car was stuck."

"You don't think my car sank yet?"

"I don't know. But—" he gazed at Boone, a surprisingly tender expression working over his features "—I have to try. I don't know how long we'll be out here tonight. Or tomorrow. Between the cold weather and all the stress, it could trigger another attack."

"I was worried about the same thing. But what about the shooter?"

"I'll do my best to stay under the radar."

How could he stay *under the radar* when he was on the bridge in the middle of the river? Fear for him sent a shiver down her limbs.

He continued. "Given that I can't contact anyone and we won't be able to get back to the ranger station tonight, we'll have to prepare to spend the night outside."

She drew in a shaky breath. That same worry had been buzzing through her mind like a horsefly in summer. Sleeping in the woods was number one on her list of I'd-rather-not activities.

"I get the sense you're not a fan of camping?"

Was she that obvious?

"Definitely not a fan. I only camped once, and it didn't go well." She closed her eyes and pressed her fingertips to her forehead to block the memories. "Actually, it was one of the worst days of my life."

"I'm sorry to hear that. Bear raid?"

"No." Lucy reopened her eyes and found him watching her closely. She sighed as the edges of those unwanted memories of her parents and their last family outing sharpened, poking her heart. "It wasn't a wild animal that caused the problems that day. It was a human-created issue."

His head cocked, his features softening with sympathy. "I wish I could say this time in the forest will be better. So far, we both know that's not the case." He looked away for a moment. "By the way, I do carry a gun, though I rarely have to use it. I'd like to show you how, just in case. If that's okay?"

She swallowed. "I guess so."

Noah withdrew the small black weapon from his side holster. He explained how to turn off the safety and hold it. Her hands trembled in his larger ones as they clasped the gun together.

"Lord willing, you won't have to use it." He set it down beside her, safety on. "Also, I need details about Boone's bag. What am I looking for?"

"His inhaler is inside his overnight bag. The bag is bright green and blue and has dinosaurs on it." Her chin quivered. "What if it's all underwater and ruined?"

"We'll cross that bridge when we come to it."

"Literally." To her surprise, Noah's mouth quirked up on one corner. Maybe he did have a sense of humor, deep down.

"Is there anything else you need from the vehicle?"

"My purse and my cell are in there. The purse is black and my cell… It fell on the driver's side floorboard when the truck slammed into us."

"If I can reach your things, I'll bring them back with me." He stood, gazing down at her with a brooding expression before withdrawing something from his pack.

"Noah?" Their eyes met, and her stomach somersaulted. "What if... What do we do if you don't return?"

"I will." He turned and set off before she had time to consider his confident words. Lucy stared at his broad back until it disappeared in the dark, then hugged Boone closer.

God, please bring him back safely. We need him.

She closed her eyes, rested her head and spine against the rock, and let the exhaustion take her.

Lucy awoke with a start. Cold air stung her cheeks, and the wind whistled through the treetops. She shivered. How long had she been asleep? The darkness surrounding her seemed unchanged, so she must have dozed off for only a few minutes. Where was Noah? Hopefully he'd return soon. Boone was limp in her arms, his breathing clear and steady.

She tried to make out the shapes around her, but the moon was hidden behind clouds. There was no way to tell the time or how long Noah had been gone. Was he okay? The thought of anything happening to him sent a painful jolt across her rib cage. Yes, this was his job, and he obviously enjoyed it, but she didn't want him hurt.

The pitch-darkness surrounding them shifted to a gauzy gray as her eyes adjusted to the night. A prickle of awareness lifted the fine hairs on her arms, then a twig snapped. Muffled panting sent an electric shock down her limbs. What—or who—was that? She inched into a more upright position and reached for the gun Noah left behind. Its cold weight felt strange in her palm.

Boone's slow, even breathing sounded

fine, but someone else nearby was breathing, too. Roughly, like the person was out of breath.

Noah? Her heart jammed in her throat, making words impossible. She aimed the gun toward the sound with shaking hands.

"There you are," a gravelly male voice taunted. "Look what you got."

A man emerged from the dark and kicked the gun from her grasp.

Noah ascended the trail beside the falls, his calves burning. Almost there. This area of the forest was one of his favorites, and he knew the path well. He slowed to catch his breath and thrust a hand through his hair. If the evening had gone as planned, he'd be leaving the ranger station right now, heading to his brother's cabin to pack, then driving five and a half hours north for a weeklong stretch alone on the AT in Virginia.

He cleared a cluster of rocks at the top with a heavy *clump*. His chest heaved from the physical exertion, and his thoughts strayed from the Appalachian Trail to the two people whose lives now depended on him.

What would've happened to Lucy and Boone if he hadn't been in the area? If he'd started his vacation a day earlier?

Thank the Lord he hadn't.

Sweat trickled down his back as he jogged down the narrow path connecting the falls hike to the Broken Branch River. Questions dogged him with each stride. Had the vehicle sunk? What if the bag holding Boone's inhaler was underwater? If he had to hike to the ranger station tonight with Boone in his arms, he could do it.

But what about Lucy?

An image of her cradling the boy came to mind. She was spirited, unafraid to question him and speak her mind—kind of like his sister. He almost smiled. No wonder she and Brielle were friends.

Another thought followed. Lucy must have a supervisor who would call her, asking how Boone was doing. Would her boss contact the police if Lucy didn't answer her phone or show up in court tomorrow or the next day?

In the distance, moonlight shone off the water. Thirty yards to go. Better check for company. Noah crouched, pulling out the binoculars stuffed into his belt bag. He set them to his face and found a clear view of the oak tree bridge.

He exhaled. Not everything was working against them tonight. The SUV's front bumper appeared to be lodged under the bridge, and the vehicle floated somehow. If he could cross the bridge, he would reach it at least.

Putting himself in full view of anyone above or from his six to ten o'clock in the woods.

God, please protect me and give me wisdom. Should I do this?

He pictured Gabriel, his critter-loving nephew. What if Jasper's son was in this predicament? Of course he'd risk it for

Gabe, and he wouldn't do any less for Boone.

He swept the area twice more. Reality was the illegal gun trafficking investigation wasn't over yet. The case wasn't closed. Shortly after Mayor David Barnhill was arrested, he had suffered a heart attack while incarcerated near Greenville. He'd died in prison, his plea deal unfinished.

It'd been a shock and a major setback for the case. Now his brother, Jasper, was returning home from his honeymoon to an even bigger mess.

He stood and shoved the binoculars back into the belt bag. How could anyone try to hurt a child like this? Boone's father had hinted to the press that someone else was involved in the illegal gun trafficking in a recent press release—had those words gotten the DA killed?

"Come on, Holt." Noah took off down the path, his gaze jumping from the trail to the shadowy woods surrounding him. He passed a large tree marked with a blaze on its trunk warning hikers they were approaching a waterway. Not that anyone could miss the sound of the steadily churning water. He unbuckled his belt bag and tucked it among the tree's root system.

After one more look around, he beelined for the bridge. The car hadn't sunk. That was a huge positive. And the bridge looked operational, at least. Still, his muscles felt tight like a Kevlar rope. He wasn't a small guy. Would his weight bring down the damaged bridge?

"God, help me, please."

The oak bridge sagged with each step. When Noah came upon the split section, he inspected the wound in the wood. It wasn't completely split. *Yet.* Once he had Lucy and Boone in a safe place, he needed to mark the bridge closed.

He crept over the broken section, moving gingerly toward the vehicle. A large hole gaped from the front windshield, and a beaver-sized clump of leaves and debris churned around the passenger side mirror. The front bumper was jammed under the bridge, lifting the backside of the vehicle up out of the water. Was it also stuck on something beneath the surface? He'd have to be careful not to knock it loose.

No time to waste.

He climbed through the railing, then stepped onto the hood. His weight pushed the vehicle lower into the water. Water splashed over his boots. He hooked his hands on the lip of the hood, where it met the windshield, then peered inside as it settled. Lucy's black purse lay on the passenger side floorboard, just like she'd said. Maybe he could grab that, too.

He scowled at the dark depths of the river. Here went nothing. Noah slid one leg into the river, gripping the passenger side mirror for stability. He flinched at the frigid water soaking his uniform pants. After a couple of seconds, the sharp sensation lessened. Suddenly his boot hit a hard surface, maybe five feet down. A branch? No, a rock. The car tires must've wedged between the bridge and a large, submerged boulder on the river bottom.

He sank his other leg into the water, setting the second boot on the underwater rock's slippery surface. The boulder shifted, and he clutched the rack on the top of the vehicle as it resettled.

His heart hammered in his chest. This wasn't the first time he'd jumped into a cold river, and it wouldn't be the last. But he'd most definitely never climbed on a half-submerged vehicle like this.

Lucy said Boone's bag was in the back seat. No way could he fit through the half-open window. It appeared the water hadn't made it in yet due to the raised position of the back end of the car. He pushed his arm through the cracked window up to his bicep. The river's continuous splashing drowned out every other sound as his fingers brushed the seats, and the bump and pull of the water made his search all the more difficult.

His lungs deflated as he felt along the back seat. No bag, no clothes. Just a soggy tissue box and a wrapper of some sort.

A gust of wind howled through the

trees, eclipsing the noise of the current. He withdrew his arm and turned, hanging heavily on the side mirror and planting his boots on the rock beneath the surface. River spray blurred his vision as he peered up at the ridge. If the shooter was nearby, most likely he'd be up there.

No sign of anyone. Noah wiped his forearm across his damp brow then shoved it back through the window. His arm felt like dead weight from the strain. Wait… *What was that?* His fingertips touched soft, scratchy material. Nylon?

Splinters of pain speared his arm as he angled his face upward and stretched. Grasping hard, he held his breath, pulling the material up to the window. The green-and-blue bag. Noah released a relieved groan. He made sure the bag was zipped then drew it through the half-open window.

After wrapping the bag's straps around his neck, he flutter-kicked closer to the bridge through the icy water, careful to keep Boone's bag from getting too wet.

With a grunt, he tossed it onto the oak bridge. His gut told him it was past time to get back to them. He turned, paddling to the front passenger window, where Lucy's purse lay on the floor. There was no way to reach her cell on the driver's side.

Noah squinted through the window.

Only way in was by breaking the glass. He reached for his baton, then scowled. He'd left it in his pack, with Lucy and Boone. Cold water bumped and pulled at his legs. The longer he stayed in the river, the bigger his concern grew about Lucy and Boone, alone.

He scrambled up and across the hood, grabbed the railing and hoisted himself onto the bridge. The frigid air, his soaked clothes, and the possibility of being shot at chilled him to his bones. He settled one of the green-and-blue bag's straps over his shoulder. His hiking boots might be waterproof against rain and mud, but they weren't meant to be completely submerged. They felt like hundred-pound rocks stuck to his feet as he made his way across the oak. The wood creaked beneath him, and liquid squished out from his socks and pants when he stepped carefully over the broken section.

Noah leaped down the bridge steps, then took off down the path. He stopped by the marked tree, snatching his belt bag from the ground, then sprinted toward the falls. No time to buckle it. The air whirred in his ears as he ran. He reached the falls and hiked down, his muscles twitching like Boone had after taking the epinephrine shot. Thank the Lord the pen had still been effective enough to help. Noah huffed. He was certain he'd checked the date on the pen recently. So how had he ended up with an expired pen?

At the bottom, he followed a different path around the plunge pool and creek than he and Lucy and Boone had taken earlier. He crisscrossed his own steps in case someone tried to tail him. About twenty yards from the area where they were hidden, he slowed to listen to the forest. The creak of tree limbs and howl of the wind through the branches were the only sounds he heard.

He made his way around the crooked stump that he'd noted on his way back to the car. It marked their hiding spot. On the other side, he stopped short, his stomach churning. His backpack sat there, but they weren't beside it.

"Lucy?"

The area was empty, the foliage trampled where they'd sat for a long period of time. Icy fingers trailed down his back. Had the shooter gotten to them?

A muffled scream tore through the underbrush. *Lucy.*

FOUR

Noah tossed Boone's bag beside his pack then took off into the woods, homing in on the location of the scream. As he closed in on Lucy's location, he slowed, moving as silently as he could. He patted his side. Where was his gun?

Her second cry hit him between the eyes, and he inched toward the sounds of a struggle up ahead.

A man stood in a clearing, a knife to Lucy's throat. "Where is the kid?"

"You're not touching him!" she shouted. "Let me go."

Noah stepped into the clearing and swept the perimeter with his gaze. No sign of his gun. "You heard her, let her go."

Her attacker spit out an oath he'd probably picked up behind bars, then scuttled backward, using her as a shield. Noah rushed him, throwing his full weight on the kidnapper. The man released Lucy and dove sideways, away from Noah. He grabbed her attacker's wrist, giving it a sharp tug. The man yelped in pain and the knife flew through the air. Lucy scrambled away, disappearing into the woods. Where was Boone?

Noah hadn't been in a real fight since his freshman year of high school, and then it had been to protect a friend. Sure, he'd gotten a three-day suspension and a black eye, but it had been worth it to stop that bully from messing with Thomas.

Thomas still recalled the fight whenever he and Noah got together to grill and shoot clays out on Thomas's property. Noah was a peaceful guy for the most part, but he'd use the Holt size and strength if a situation called for it. And this one did.

Noah chased him down and swept the man's feet, sending him to the ground.

The man rolled away then grabbed a large stick, brandishing it like a baseball bat.

"I wouldn't get in the middle of this," he growled as he lumbered to his feet. "He's not gonna stop!"

Noah dodged the swinging stick, landing a jab to the man's ribs. The wood weapon thumped into Noah's shoulder, and he ducked away from it then sent a punch at the man's face. It wasn't a hard hit, but Lucy's attacker cried out and crumpled to the ground.

Noah looked wildly around. How could he restrain the man? His gun was MIA and his cuffs were in his backpack. Suddenly the man rose to his hands and knees and crawled around a large stump. Darkness swallowed the criminal whole, and the heavy, uneven sound of thudding footsteps followed. He was getting away. Noah launched after him, but several strides in he pulled up short.

He couldn't chase the man down now. Lucy and Boone needed him.

Noah growled, then turned, jogging

back toward where Lucy had run off. His mind filed away the specifics of the would-be kidnapper. He was five-seven, maybe five-eight, and one-ninety at least. Late thirties or early forties, though it was tough to tell. Dark hair, balding on top. Camo-style clothing.

"Lucy?"

Soft crying brought him out of cataloging the details. *Boone. Or Lucy?* He strode through the foliage trampled from their fight, and the glint of silver caught his gaze. He sank to his knees. The man's knife lay across a stick, long and deadly.

He needed one of the evidence bags from his pack in case fingerprints were salvageable on the knife's handle. Noah spun in a circle to memorize the area, then searched for Lucy and Boone.

He found Boone against a boulder, his legs drawn to his chest. Lucy huddled at his side, murmuring to the boy. They were close to the original hiding spot.

"I tried to use the gun, but he kicked it away before I could." She looked up at him with red-rimmed eyes. "Is he still out there?"

"No. He took off. Left his knife on the ground. I'm going to retrieve it as evidence."

She nodded, drawing in her bottom lip. In the dim light, he could make out dirt streaked on her face, and was that blood?

"Are either of you hurt?"

"He didn't get me," Boone whispered.

Lucy shook her head no, but her rapid breathing and shivering body told him a different story. She was in shock once again. He kneeled to inspect her face.

"You have a cut here." He gently touched the skin near her chin. Her dark eyes widened as he cupped her face with his palms. "He must've nicked you with the knife. That's the only wound I see."

She reached up to touch the same spot on her jawbone, then winced. "I think that's from his fingernail, when he first grabbed me."

"I'm sorry he touched you at all." Noah contemplated the man's verbal threat.

Now wasn't the time to share what the attacker had said. Lucy and Boone were scared enough.

I wouldn't get in the middle of this... He's not gonna stop.

Who was *he*? It must be the man who killed Boone's father and attempted to murder his mother. Was it one man...or more?

She blinked up at him. "Are you hurt?"

"No. I'm good. Here." He stood and grabbed Boone's bag, then handed it to her. She clutched the bag and let out a sigh of relief. He reached for his pack and dug out an evidence bag. "Make sure the inhaler is inside. I'll be right back."

He pushed through the trees. When he came upon the area where they'd fought, Noah searched for the knife. *There.* It glinted in the moonlight. He retrieved the weapon with a rag inside the bag, then sealed the container. After one last inspection of the area, he jogged back to the boulder where they waited.

Two things were clear. Whoever was

after Boone wasn't going to give up easily. And by protecting the boy, Lucy had become a target, too.

Which meant he was their only hope of getting out of the forest alive.

Lucy followed closely as Noah led them toward the waterfall. Her muscles were still rubbery and her mouth bone-dry from the attack. Darkness closed in on them as clouds concealed the moon again. She crossed her arms, rubbing them to ward off goose bumps. Noah was right. It kept getting colder. It didn't help that as they approached the waterfall again, the spray misted the air, dampening her hair and cheeks.

He reassured her there was a hiding spot near the falls where they would be safe overnight.

After he scoured the area and found the gun, Noah had lifted Boone into his arms, joking that they were in stealth mode and couldn't make much noise. Hopefully the child would fall back asleep and forget the nightmare of what almost happened.

She shuddered. All she could think about was the thick, snakelike arms of her and Boone's attacker as the man tried to drag them apart. When she was on the ground, he'd searched the area intently for something. Noah's gun? Or maybe for Boone, who had darted behind a tree trunk to hide.

They slipped through a wall of tall, thin trees. The sound of splashing water increased, which meant they were getting close. Good. Her ankle boots sank into the cold, uneven ground and slid on slick leaves until her toes cried out for relief from the constricting leather shoes she used to believe were comfortable.

"Are you doing okay?" Noah swiveled around like she'd spoken her thoughts out loud.

"I'd like to rip these shoes off and throw them into the water."

He frowned down at her feet. "You can take them off when we get to the cave."

Cave. The word didn't inspire much relief or excitement. Still, it meant protection from the elements. Boone desperately needed that.

The path wound around the large pool at the base of the waterfall. Noah led them toward a dark hole up ahead. That must be the cave entrance.

"It's about twenty yards deep. Might be bats but shouldn't be anything else alive in there."

Lucy raked her fingernails across her palms. "Bats?"

"They'd be roosting anyway, since it's winter."

Was that supposed to make her feel better? "Okay."

"Too many hikers frequent this spot for bears to den up here." He leaned over, looking at the ground.

What was he checking for, footprints?

Boone lay peacefully in Noah's arms, his head nestled against Noah's chest. *Sweet boy.* What a traumatic evening.

Lucy understood his exhaustion. She felt

like a walking dishrag—limp, her clothes soggy from the river and the muddy ground, and weak from the stress of the evening's terrible events.

Noah turned to face her. "Can you hold him for a few seconds while I check inside?"

"Of course."

He passed Boone off to her, and she settled his weight against her as Noah treaded into the cave.

Boone shifted, raising his head. "Where is Mr. Noah?"

"He's making sure the cave is clear. He'll be right back." She understood Boone's uneasiness. She didn't want Noah far away, either. There was no way they would've survived out here without him.

"We get to sleep in a cave tonight." Normally the thought of being inside a dank, smelly cave would've sent her running. But after being out in the wind and cold for so long, she was ready to get inside and close her eyes.

Noah reappeared, his large, silent form

giving her a start. He noticed, muttering, "Sorry. All good. Dry, at least. There are a couple logs people have set up for sitting on. You can prop yourselves against that and try to sleep." He squinted down at Boone. "Hey, buddy, you up for sleeping on the ground like a real outdoorsman?"

Boone yawned, then melted into Lucy. "Mhm."

"I feel the same." Lucy tried to work up a smile.

Noah tousled the boy's hair softly, meeting Lucy's gaze then slipping his arm through hers. "It's pitch-dark in here. It'll take a minute for your eyes to adjust, and it's still dark even then."

As he led her inside, the darkness intensified, until an ebony curtain dropped in front of her. The air moistened, a cloying scent of decay and dirt lingering.

"I'm scared." Boone's body pressed into hers.

"Shh, it's okay," Lucy soothed. "We're right here with you. Mr. Noah got your bag. Why don't we get your clothes changed so you aren't wet anymore? You'll be cozier then."

"I'll take him so you can get his stuff out." Noah leaned in, retrieving Boone.

Once her arms were free, she opened Boone's bag and fished around for clean clothes. Her fingers brushed hard plastic and a couple little figurines. Toys and electronic gadgets. *There.* Clothing. Thick, long-sleeved pajamas. A soft ball of clean socks. Noah set Boone down, and they helped him change in the pitch-dark. When he finished, she bundled up his ruined clothes.

"Here, I'll lay out his jeans to dry. The rest can go in this bag." Noah took the small wad and crinkling ensued. Then he zipped something—his backpack, she'd guess.

"Good idea to dry his jeans."

"He'll need them tomorrow," Noah said. "Do you want to sit down so you can take off your shoes? Just move slow so you don't bump into the wall."

She felt around to situate herself. The

ground was hard, and small clumps of grit stuck to her pants and palms as she sat down. Lucy unzipped her ankle boots and pulled them off. She released a grateful sigh. Along with shelter and food, finding dry socks and a better pair of hiking shoes—the one type of shoe she'd never wanted—was important. She snorted.

"Something funny?" Noah asked as he placed Boone on her lap. The child squirmed, clearly happy to be out of the dirty, damp clothes. And fighting sleep. She rubbed Boone's back until his breathing settled into the calm cadence of deep sleep.

"Nothing is actually funny," she answered. "It's more like irony. I've never, ever, wanted hiking boots, because I don't hike. But right now I'd give my life savings for a pair. Used, new. I don't care."

He grunted in answer. Of course. She chuckled.

"And now I'm laughing because somehow I—we—ended up with a man of few words." She lightly poked her elbow to-

ward the sound of his breathing, then startled when it connected with his ribs. He
was sitting down now, too, right next to
her.

"I'm sorry." She pulled her elbow back
and slumped over. "I feel very lost not
knowing what's going on or what's coming next."

"I understand. I don't know exactly
what's coming next, either," he admitted,
then paused. "But I'm working out a plan.
Is he asleep?"

"I think so."

"This is a dangerous, moment-by-mo-
ment situation," Noah murmured. "Anyone would feel lost. Scared. Would you
like me to hash out the details of my
plan?"

Was he making fun of her? Her backbone straightened. "If we're talking about
the life of this sweet child and, if I'm
being honest, my own, then yes. I would
like that." She tucked her bottom lip as the
neediness of her plea fell on her own ears.
She didn't consider herself high-mainte-

nance, but in this situation, she must appear that way to Noah Holt.

"Anything to help you feel safer."

The fight left her spine. He wasn't making fun. "It's just that I'm not used to someone else taking charge of my life. Making decisions for me. I'm pretty independent."

"I can see that. You did a great job protecting Boone back there."

Her cheeks warmed at his sincere praise.

"I'm here to get you two out of the forest alive, not take charge of your life." He shifted his position so he was even closer. "Go ahead, ask me whatever you want."

Tears prickled her eyes at his unexpected kindness. Her dad had left after her parents' divorce, and she seemed to possess a broken radar for whether men were teasing her or being unkind. Micah, her brother, had been an unusually serious child, so that relationship hadn't helped.

"How many times have you been in this cave?"

"Dozens. Maybe fifty. I've never slept inside here, though."

"You must be able to walk these woods blindfolded."

"I'd rather not. I enjoy the view too much."

She smiled. They were so different. All she ever wanted when she drove from the courthouse to her apartment was to hurry through the forest. He adored the woods and spent most of his time here. "How long have you worked as a forest ranger?"

"I've been at this section of Sumter for almost six years. I was a ranger near the coast, in the Francis Marion National Forest, for two years before transferring to be closer to my family."

"Family? Brielle and your police officer brother?"

"And my mom. Dana." He shifted his feet. "I thought this discussion was about my plans to keep you two safe?"

"Right. So, what's the plan?"

"First, you sleep. You're both exhausted from all the adrenaline your body used tonight. Boone needs to stay still long enough to get some rest. You do, too. No one can reach us here, by air or road. So tomorrow we're guaranteed to spend all day hiking, and for that you'll need energy. Lots of it."

It was the longest chunk of words she'd heard him string together all night.

And he was right. Her body felt like it'd been shoved in a washing machine and placed on spin cycle. Poor Boone must feel the same way.

"Tomorrow," he continued, "we'll head out at first light. There's an old ranger cabin not too far. Should have supplies, and hopefully along the way I can reach Derek on the radio."

"There's food?" Her stomach growled as if on cue. She cringed.

"I hope there are rations at the cabin. If nothing else, there will be canned food. We'll have to eat it cold. I have some jerky and trail mix left, but not a lot. That will be breakfast tomorrow."

He made a noise like he was stretching, then his arm lined up beside hers and stayed there. "Don't expect gourmet food."

"I'm considering eating moss right now, thank you very much."

"Let's pray it doesn't come to that." He sat forward and reached out, then she heard his pack unzipping. Moments later he pressed a strip of jerky into her hand. "Sounds like you need this."

"Thanks." She bit off a piece, chewing vigorously on the salty meat. Outside the wind stirred up, howling, and the sudden, heavy *patter* of rain carried in. "I feel dumb about losing your gun when the man came after us."

"Don't feel dumb." He put the food back. "I found it, and everything turned out okay. You kept Boone safe, Lucy. You were pretty brave out there."

Brave. No one had ever called her that before. Noah's words settled inside the cold parts of her like warm tea.

He continued. "Once we leave the cabin, there's a field about a half mile past it where a helicopter should be able to land. It's near the fire tower, which is a well-known location. Should be able to rendez-vous with police there. Also, the ranger cabin might have extra hiking boots, but I can't guarantee they'll fit."

"I'll take what I can get. Believe it or not, those are my most comfortable work shoes." She scooched down to alleviate a kink in her lower back. Boone rolled off her, nestling between them. "It'll be like Christmas morning if there's a pair at the cabin that fit."

Noah chuckled. "Can't believe Christmas is three weeks away."

"Me, either. Will you celebrate with your family? Your brother?"

"And Kinsley, his wife. Their son, Gabe. My mom, too. Hopefully Brielle will show up. How about you?"

"I might go see my brother." She choked down the last bite of jerky. Thinking about Christmases past always brought painful memories to mind. Noah handed her the thermos, his attentiveness a balm for her aching heart. "Coming here was a good idea."

"I'm full of them." He paused. "Good ideas."

"You definitely are." She blinked rapidly as the urge to lay her head on his shoulder pulled at her. "Thank you for going back to get Boone's inhaler."

"I'm just grateful I could get to it."

She handed him the thermos. "Once we're to the cabin, what's next?"

"I'll try to reach Derek and the Tunnel Creek PD." He rifled through his pockets.

"Speaking of that, how do we know who to trust in all this? Didn't a police officer get arrested in the gun smuggling ring?"

"Yes." He ground out the word, and she frowned. Had Noah known the man?

"Dean wasn't really a friend, but my brother and I knew him a long time. Went to high school and played ball with him. It was a real gut punch finding out he'd gotten involved."

"I'm sorry. Is there... Do you think

there are still criminals loose who are involved?"

"After what happened to Ryan, Boone's father, and now to you both, yes. I do." He paused. "And whoever is still involved is determined to eliminate the threat."

Lucy shivered, dropping her voice to a whisper. "I can't wrap my mind around what these men would want with a child."

"My guess is they think he heard something incriminating or saw one of their faces."

"He was asleep in his bedroom on the second floor. At least, that's what Melissa told the judge."

"Who's Melissa?"

"My supervisor."

"Okay. Hey, why don't you try to get some rest?" Noah sounded weary. "You're only going to be sleeping a few hours. Here." He set his broad shoulder against hers. "Lean on me."

Lean on me. Had Lucy ever been able to lean on anyone in her life? No one she could recall.

The wind whipped through the trees outside the cave, the sound of the rain mixing with the waterfall's thunder. She leaned on Noah, her insides shaking like the branches outside. Even in semi-sleep, a dark question formed behind her closed eyelids—would they make it to the ranger cabin without that man finding them again?

Noah shifted at the cave's entrance, tracing the dirt with his boot. Puddles marked the path outside, and cold air seeped over him. Faint light spilled into the dark orifice they'd slept in, but still he couldn't find what he was missing.

He shoved his hands into his pockets. Where had he dropped the belt bag that held his cell and the binoculars? He racked his brain trying to remember when he'd had it last. While running toward Lucy's attacker? Or when he was jogging back from the river?

Either way, it was out there somewhere. And until he found the belt bag, his cell and binoculars were missing. He kicked a stone into the weeds. At least he still had his gun and the radio.

Without his watch, he had to guess the time. It looked to be around 7:00 a.m., if he was reading the sky correctly. This time of year, the sun rose slowly, like it was cold, too. He loved winter, though not when he was stuck outside without a choice of returning to his warm bed.

He glanced back at Lucy and Boone. The boy lay with his head on Lucy's middle, and his breathing was slow and clear, praise God. For now, the asthma wasn't bothering him.

After sleeping a few hours, Noah had set up a vigil at the cave's entrance. Questions hounded him like Jasper's two redbone coonhounds after a raccoon. When the gun trafficking ring Jasper uncovered was laid bare, multiple men had been arrested. Sure, Mayor Barnhill's death was bad news for the investigation, but the charges were nearly certain for the others. Still, someone *else* must've escaped the figurative fire then disappeared before the feds were able to tie in any connections.

But who? And did the criminals-at-large really believe Boone would recognize their voices? He was five years old, with a child's attention span and probably a spotty memory.

Noah paced. His pants had dried overnight, and he worked the stiffness out of the material. He was antsy to try his radio again, but it would wake up Boone and Lucy, and they needed as much rest as possible.

Sleeping under the stars was one of his favorite activities, but last night was different. He felt unprepared caring for—and protecting—two additional people with his meager supplies.

A soft rustle sounded behind him, and he turned. Lucy was slowly sitting up, rubbing her eyes.

He gave the woods one last look, then pivoted and treaded toward her. With the sun rising, the cave entrance would be fully illuminated and their hiding spot more obvious if the shooter was still after them.

"Hey, did you get some sleep?" He crouched beside them. Boone was out cold, curled on his side. Lucy stroked the boy's back tenderly.

"I think. Except it felt like five minutes. What about you? Did you sleep?"

"Little bit." Not nearly enough, but he'd sleep later. "Something's come up."

"What now?" Her hand stilled on Boone's shoulder.

"My phone is missing." He stood, releasing a pent-up breath. "I either dropped it when I went to the river, or as that man and I fought. I need to go back to see if it's there. If the radio doesn't work, the cell might be our only chance of getting a hold of authorities."

She nodded. "Should I wait here with Boone?"

The child rustled, letting out a sleepy groan and stretching his body out like Jasper's son, Gabe, often did. Lucy stood, doing the same.

He averted his gaze. "No, I don't want to leave you again. Let's eat something, get Boone back in his jeans, then head toward the area where you were attacked. I'll make it quick. If it's not there, it's possible there's an extra burner phone at the cabin."

"Whoa, I never slept outside before." Boone's round brown eyes took in the cave in awe.

She combed down his messy hair then pulled them both up to standing. "And hopefully we don't have to do that again."

Her dislike of the outdoors made him curious. She said last night she'd never wanted hiking boots. What happened on that ill-fated camping trip? Noah shook off the question then reached into his pack, doling out the trail mix and one piece of jerky each. Boone wolfed down the handful. Guilt stung Noah like a bee because he couldn't offer them anything else. After they ate, he shared his thermos and invited them to take a few large swallows.

"It's cold out there, but we still have to stay hydrated." At her questioning look, he explained, "I have a filtering device I can use to refill the thermos. There's a creek about three-quarters of a mile away."

She nodded, then caught her hair into a knot at the base of her neck. "So we're going to look for your belt bag, and then to the ranger cabin?"

"Yes. The ranger cabin is the closest safe structure. We should be able to make it to the cabin by midday, and I'll see how the weather is and if I can finally get reception. This time tomorrow you two should be under police protection."

She was quiet compared to last night. "Will your brother be involved in the case, then?"

"Not yet. He won't get back for a couple days."

"What about you?"

Noah shook his head. "While I can make arrests, it's typically for poaching or dumping or some kind of land violation. I don't investigate crimes. The Tunnel Creek Police Department does that. Sometimes the feds get involved, which very well may happen with this case."

"The police?" Boone circled Lucy's leg then threw his head back. "Do I *have* to talk to them more?"

Noah dropped to his heels in front of Boone. "My brother is a police officer. He's a good guy, I promise. You'll be safe there."

"The cars are loud. They came after Mommy yelled at the bad man, then he went *boom*."

Noah glanced up to meet Lucy's eyes. Maybe the boy knew more than they thought.

Lucy crouched in front of Boone, too, cupping the child's shoulders. "What do you mean, Mommy yelled at the bad man?"

"Mommy yelled at a man and he yelled at her. Then it went *boom*. I went to my closet 'cause I was scared." He bobbed back and forth in a wiggly dance. "I have to go potty."

Noah helped Boone take care of necessities and change into his mostly dry jeans, then he gathered his pack and the blanket, wrapping the material back around Boone and slinging the pack on. He made sure his weapon was secure, and the three of them headed out. No one said a word as they exited the cave. Usually being out on a trail cleared his mind, but today was different. Way different. His questions and worries compounded with each stride.

Boone was a witness to a murder and an attempted murder. Or at least the criminals who perpetrated the crime believed so.

The man or men after Boone and now Lucy were not going to give up in their pursuit, even in a national forest.

Noah's jaw ticked. And he would go to any lengths to protect them.

FIVE

Lucy trailed after Noah as they hiked toward a rocky outcrop. The ranger's frustration was palpable in his fast stride and the set of his broad shoulders. He hadn't been able to locate his belt bag.

In the daylight, the crushed plants and trampled ground where she and Boone were attacked last night sent a shiver through her. Noah searched for several minutes, pushing through thickets and kicking beneath dead branches and mounds of wet red and brown leaves.

Afterward he hefted Boone onto his back and set off. His pace kept her pulse humming. Sunlight flickered through the bare trees in gold shadows, and the air was sharp and cold after last night's storm. A cardinal crossed the pathway, letting out a series of high-pitched chirps.

If they weren't being chased by a man with a gun, she might agree with Noah about this area. It *was* beautiful. Peaceful, even. Which was strange, because usually the woods gave her claustrophobia. Heart-racing anxiety. Which had started after the one and only camping trip her family had taken. Where her mom and dad fought the whole time, then left on a hike, not returning for several hours. Nearly half a day. Lucy and her brother, Micah, had wandered the campsite and cried in their tents, calling for their parents and arguing about what to do.

The heel of her ankle boot slipped on a large stone, and she stumbled forward.

"Hey, you okay?" Noah slowed.

"Just tired." The lie came easily. Noah loved the outdoors and his job. He of all people wouldn't understand her discomfort and fear upon entering the woods.

They resumed climbing the steep, rock-laden trail, and she focused on Boone and

Noah's banter so she didn't think about her ankle boots sawing into her heels while compacting her toes into tiny nubs.

He and Boone tease-boasted about who could hike around the world the fastest. She smiled.

Sorry, Boone, but Mr. Super Ranger would win that one.

An overwhelming urge to stay with Noah instead of relying on authorities caught her by surprise. Maybe if his police officer brother were there, she'd trust the situation more. But he wasn't, and Lucy dreaded the thought of leaving Noah's side. In the short time they'd been together, he'd proven he was well qualified to look out for them.

That he would protect them at any cost.

"I'm hungry," Boone whined.

Noah set him down then unzipped his pack, tugging out a small container. More beef jerky. Still, her stomach grumbled at the sight of the skinny brown sticks of meat she used to avoid at the grocery store.

Boone clutched the food, taking bite after bite, chewing until his cheeks resembled a chipmunk's. Noah passed him the thermos, then offered Lucy a piece of jerky.

"What do you say?" she prompted the boy.

"Thank you," Boone mumbled through his full mouth.

Noah murmured, "You're welcome," then addressed Lucy. "Want to take a fiver?"

"If a fiver means we stop, then yes, please."

"A fiver means a five-minute break."

They sat side by side on a large rock. Boone finished eating then squatted on the ground in front of them, collecting sticks. Good thing Noah had thought to spread Boone's jeans out last night to dry. Her slacks were stiff but dry as well. Lucy unzipped then tugged off her ankle boots. The cool air felt wonderful on her tortured feet.

Noah's watchful gaze roamed the area.

Winter had clearly arrived. Many of the trees were bare, the leaves littering the earth in a carpet of brown, yellow and red. A prickle of unease lodged between her shoulder blades. Did that mean it was easier to see them now?

"Do you think the...person from yesterday is still around?" she asked Noah.

"I'm not sure." His brows arched. "My biggest concern is that he might've gone back for reinforcements."

A chill swept over her body. What if he was right and more men were coming after them?

She focused on Boone and his armful of sticks. "What are you doing, Mr. Explorer?"

"Collecting wood for a fire." He added to his haphazard pile. "See how many?"

"That big pile would keep me warm all day. Too bad we can't burn it now." She turned to find Noah's eyes on her.

"You're really good with him." He nodded at Boone, now counting his twig treasure. "Is that why you became a caseworker? You like working with kids?"

"That, and because I know what it's like to have your family broken apart." She looked away from him. "To feel completely abandoned."

Noah didn't say anything, and his unhurried silence prompted her to continue.

"My dad was a truck driver, and my mom was—still is—a nurse. Right after my tenth birthday, they separated. Happy birthday, right? They divorced a few months later. Dad had another significant other, and he left us to move across the country with her. My mom…" Lucy threaded her fingers so tightly her knuckles turned white. "Mom kind of fell apart after that. She disappeared for days at a time. Then she'd reappear and tell us how sorry she was. We always covered for her."

He gazed at her with more sympathy than she knew what to do with.

"The last time, my brother and I were maybe eleven and thirteen. Micah, my brother, tried to play it off like she had extra hours at the hospital, but I heard him when he called her shift manager to ask if our mom was there. He was worried. Scared. We had barely any food left in our fridge. My mom hadn't come into work for her shift. Her manager called the authorities, and we were taken into foster care after that."

"I'm sorry, Lucy." He whistled softly. "That sounds brutal."

She gave a weak shrug. "It was."

"Are you close to your brother?"

"We talk once or twice a week." The cold rock bored into her backside, and Lucy stood, rubbing her arms. "Micah is an ophthalmologist in Greenville. He's married now, and they're expecting a baby in a few months."

"You don't sound happy about it."

Instead of making her defensive, Noah's gentle words settled the hurt swirling in her chest. There was an underlying question there, a sincerity that surprised her.

She could tell he cared enough to want to understand her emotions.

"I'm happy for them. Trish is a sweetheart. I just don't understand how he can do that after what we went through. It seems like too much of a risk to me."

Noah's intense hazel eyes pinned hers. "You don't want to get married and have a family one day?"

"No. I saw my mom fade into a shadow of who she was after my dad left." She swallowed a lump that felt like an entire jerky stick stuck in her throat. "When you deal with what I went through, feeling alone and abandoned, it damages something inside you."

"What if *having* a family would help heal that?"

She shook her head. "How can I risk putting a child—my child—through that?"

Noah started to say more but then stopped. He pushed off the rock and stared up through the trees. "We may have company."

"What do you mean?" Her heart flip-flopped.

"Hear that?" He pointed to the sky. A low whirring sound burned her ears.

A helicopter?

"The question is, are they here to help?" Noah reached back, then scowled as he remembered his binoculars weren't there. Normally choppers didn't fly through this area unless a hiker was lost or there was a fire. Clearly a fire wasn't an issue—he would've smelled it, and the ground was saturated after multiple storms. Which meant it was possible word had gotten out about Lucy and Boone's disappearance. Maybe it was Tunnel Creek PD?

He set a hand to his brow and squinted. The bird closed in, until he could make out more details. Sleek black with silver trim, no identifiable logo across the side or front. One male figure manned the controls while another stood in the opening on the side, a long black—

The *zing-zing* of bullets sent a current

of shock through his nerves. A sniper rifle. Lucy screamed. Noah hefted Boone, wrapped an arm around Lucy and dove into a thick hedge behind the rock.

That was no police helicopter.

His face and neck stung from the collision with the sharp branches. He wedged them deeper in between the rock and the bushes, listening intently. The chopper had flown past. Would it circle back?

"They're not here to help," Lucy panted, her face mashed into his neck.

"No, they're not." Were they hidden enough? His gut clenched.

While his brownish-green uniform would camouflage well enough, Boone's bright green-and-blue bag would flag down the men.

"Make sure Boone's bag is hidden. Shove it underneath your legs."

She did as he asked, squirming to push the bag under her. Noah tugged out his radio and tried to reach Derek again.

"This is Brown Tree. Over."

Crackling static filled the air, eclipsing

the noise from the helicopter's blades in the distance. He tried again, but still no answer. Noah clicked it off. The man who attacked Lucy and Boone had done exactly what he worried about—brought in help.

"They're coming back. Hold still." The whirring noise increased as the chopper flew closer, creating a roaring wind that flattened everything in a fifty-yard radius. Including the bushes they were tucked beneath.

Please, God, keep us hidden.

The helicopter circled two more times, then flew off. He waited for a couple of minutes, then peered from behind the rock. It sounded like the chopper had headed east. Toward town, where they had taken off? Whose chopper was that? He'd never seen it before.

"Are they gone?" Lucy asked.

"Looks that way." He adjusted his position so they could get out from the bushes. Boone crawled to Lucy's side, and started clutching at his bag.

The muffled sound of a barking dog startled Noah. "What was that?"

"Was that a dog?" Lucy sat up. "It's not coming from your radio?"

"No. That's not me." His throat closed. Had they sent tracking dogs?

Boone tapped Noah's arm. "It's my voice recorder, Mr. Barkey."

Lucy tilted her head. "Is it coming from your bag?"

"Yeah. Mr. Barkey is my toy. Mommy put our dog, Sammy, on Mr. Barkey."

"Must be a recording device." Noah blew out a hard breath. "My nephew, Gabe, has something similar."

Boone nodded with his whole body. "Mommy got it for my birthday so I could hear Sammy all the time I want to."

Lucy glanced at Noah. She must be thinking the same thought he was. Thank the Lord it wasn't tracking dogs. But they needed to turn the toy off. Noah unzipped Boone's bag. He located a hard, rounded plastic object and pulled it out.

A small white toy animal filled his

palm. About five inches tall and three inches wide, the plastic dog had a black collar and red fabric tongue sticking out.

"This is Mr. Barkey?"

"Uh-huh. Listen." The child pushed something on the bottom, and a dog's barking sounded again. Noah knew dogs well enough to gather the bark was from a small dog. A terrier or miniature pinscher.

He inspected the dog toy. Its triangular ears were speakers, and underneath were the three buttons that must play the sounds.

Boone's face fell. "I miss Sammy."

Lucy patted his shoulder. "When we get out of the woods, you can see Sammy again."

Noah used his thumbnail to click the power button off. He set it back into the bag, then rose cautiously, scanning the horizon. No sign of the helicopter, but another storm blowing in from the west filled the horizon, a massive wall of churning gray clouds coming their way.

"I think we're safe to move, but we have

to hurry. That cold front is intensifying."
If they weren't out in the woods, running for their lives, he'd pray for some snow. An early Christmas dusting. But that would only complicate their current situation.

He helped them to their feet then swiped off bits of dirt and moss from his pants. Lucy did the same. A tiny stick stuck out of her dark hair, and Noah reached over to pull it out.

"Sorry—this is stuck."

Her eyes rounded as he focused on the twig near her ear. "See?" He held it out between them, then tossed it to the earth.

"Thank you." She looked down, then back up at him. "You're bleeding a little." She used her fingertip to dab a spot on his forehead, then another.

"It's probably from the bushes." Their gazes collided. Heat climbed his neck. What was going on? Lucy was a citizen in his care. That was it. He shook it off. "Ready to move?"

Lucy nodded, and they fell into a single file line. He led their mismatched hiking party over the next mountain. Then into the valley below. The wind whistled through the bare branches, the mournful sound raising goose bumps along his arms. He kept an eagle eye on the sky, especially when they pushed past the rocky outcropping marking the entrance to the Ellicott Rock Wilderness area. The eight-thousand-acre natural area was one of his favorites to hike. It was close to the Blue Ridge Mountain line and the busiest area for tourists. But this time of year, hikers were rare and often he'd go hours without running into anyone.

He tried his radio three times over the next hour, in three different spots. Three elevations. Nothing. Why wasn't Derek answering? He pushed a branch back to allow Lucy and Boone through without getting whacked by it. Derek had dealt with a bad breakup a couple months ago. That could be why he was out of communication, too. He'd been kind of withdrawn and distracted since it happened.

Derek's office was at the Buckhead ranger station outside Tunnel Creek. Normally reception was excellent there. Noah tried Shawn Baxter's signal, too, to no avail. Shawn was new but seemed eager to get involved and learn the ropes. Still, each attempt to reach them ended with more static.

On top of that, he couldn't stop thinking about Lucy's words earlier. It took a lot to surprise him, and she'd done it. She loved kids, but didn't want any of her own. The thought made him strangely sad.

Lucy and Boone struggled to keep up. He was hungry, bordering on ravenous, and no doubt they were as well. Lord willing, the ranger cabin was stocked with extra food. Even a can of beans sounded good right now.

The chill in the air followed them along the range line. By the sun's position in the sky, it was nearing noon or later. And the clouds he had seen in the distance were closing in. They had one, maybe two hours before more rain arrived. He could smell it on the wind.

His thoughts switched to Lucy's cell phone, which remained in her car on the Broken Branch River. Had anyone tried calling or texting her yet? Did they wonder why she hadn't responded? Had her supervisor heard from the judge?

"How is his mother doing?" He turned, flicking his eyes toward Boone.

"Last I heard, she was stable. There is... hope, I think."

"I'm glad. I'll pray for that."

"Thank you. Yes, we should do that. Pray." She seemed to consider the word for a few seconds. "Do you think the police will...keep her safe...where she is right now?" She mouthed the word *hospital* at him.

"In a case like this, I'd assume so. I'll ask that question as soon as I get in contact with someone."

She leaned forward to catch her breath. "Any chance we can take a fiver?"

He chuckled at her easy use of the hiking term. She had soldiered through the last few hours of hiking in her fancy city boots—plus the unexpected attack from the sky—without a complaint. And won his respect in the process.

"Yes, we can stop here."

Noah ushered them off the path, through a break in the tree line. He chose an area with a high, dense canopy so they weren't sitting ducks this time. Lucy pulled off her shoes and wiggled her toes at Boone. The little boy giggled as she pretended her feet were attacking him.

He kept an ear and eye out for any company. So far he'd seen nothing suspicious on the ground. No footsteps in mud, no signs of other human life. Good thing, because they were close to the ranger cabin. It sat on the other side of the ridge they were traversing.

"There's about an hour left." If he'd been hiking alone, he'd be there in twenty-five minutes, give or take a few. But he had to cut his pace significantly to accommodate Boone's short legs and Lucy's limping stride. Hopefully they'd find some better footwear for her to wear. *And* he'd be able to call in for help.

Noah tweaked the boy's arm as Boone poked at clumps of moss on a stump. "Can I ask you something about the bad night?"

Boone didn't respond at first. His refusal to make eye contact told Noah the boy would much rather not talk about what happened. He'd likely been questioned for hours by police and social workers after the incident at his house.

"Do you have to?"

"I do. It won't be a lot of questions. Just two." He ruffled Boone's hair. "I work in the woods, but I'm a law enforcement ranger. Kind of like a police officer in the trees."

Boone looked up at him. "That's why your name's Brown Tree on the radio? And because you're tall?"

"Yep. That's right." He squatted so they were eye-to-eye. "The first question is, did you see the bad men when they came in your house or when they left?"

Boone squished his lips up and out, tilting his head, then shaking it back and forth. *No.*

"Just one more question. Do you remember what the bad man yelled at your mom?"

"Uh-huh. He said *give it to me*." Boone raised his hand and pointed his fingers like a gun. "Then it went *boom* and I ran in my closet so fast."

Noah and Lucy made eye contact over his head. Noah blinked at this news. What was the murderer looking for at the Harringtons' house?

They continued hiking, Lucy offering to carry his backpack while he carried Boone. Once they were past the ridgeline, the woods split and the rustic brown ranger cabin came into view.

"That's it."

He scanned the woods and the small clearing around the structure, his skin tingling with awareness. Lord willing, no one else had found it first. Especially the man who'd attacked them yesterday.

SIX

Lucy crouched beside a tree with Boone as Noah trudged ahead to inspect the nondescript building. It sat in a clearing and resembled a shack more than a cabin, but it had a roof, two windows and, from what she could see, a front door. Most importantly, food.

When he opened the door and strode inside, gun drawn, she held her breath.

"There he goes," she whispered. The wind tugged hair loose from her messy bun, sending strands across her face. She tucked them behind her ears and shivered. The clouds he'd pointed out earlier were almost overhead. The sun was long gone, and the cold air stung her eyes.

Boone pushed up against her side. "Is the bad guy in there?"

"No, I don't think so." She curled her arm around his shoulder. "He's just checking to make sure—"

Static flooded her eardrums, then someone's voice came over Noah's radio.

"Brown Tree, come in. Brown Tree. Come in. Over."

Lucy gasped. Someone was trying to reach him! They must be in a better spot for reception. What should she do? Noah was far enough away and inside that he most likely couldn't hear it.

Boone watched with wide eyes as she pulled the radio out of Noah's bag and switched the button on, then pushed talk. "This is Brown Tree." She felt silly saying his call name but she needed them to know they'd reached Noah.

Silence dragged on for several seconds before a voice returned to the line. "Who is this? Identify yourself. Over."

"This is Brown Tree." She licked her lips, glanced at Boone. "Over."

"This isn't Brown Tree. Where is Ranger Holt? Over."

"He's here. Copy. Whatever." Her mind scrambled. "He's looking at the cabin, but we're with him." That didn't make sense. How could she tell the man where they were?

"Who's we? Which cabin? Please identify yourself. Over."

Noah appeared in the cabin's door, motioning at her. She leaped to her feet and waved the radio. "Someone is on this! They're trying to reach you."

He sprinted over. "What's going on?" He grabbed the radio and pushed the button. "This is Brown Tree. Over."

"Copy. Brown Tree, this is Black Bird. That you? Over."

"Copy. Woman and child were in a car accident last night. Broken Branch Ridge. Vehicle in the river. No injuries but we need assistance. Over."

"Copy that."

Noah continued, "Where is Red Knight? Over."

"Red Knight not available. What's your location for assistance? Over."

Noah started to speak then stopped, and his gaze connected to hers. Was that hesitation in his eyes?

"Meet at Middle Valley. East of the fire tower on Lookout Mountain. Oh-900 tomorrow. Over."

There was a minute of silence before the person's voice—Black Bird—came back on the line and repeated what Noah had said, then finished with, "Copy."

Noah clicked off the device, then retrieved his pack. He motioned them to the cabin, but not before she noticed a troubled expression on his face.

They entered the front door and he shut it behind them, then Noah handed her the thermos. She took a long drink and looked around before meeting his eyes. A musty smell wrinkled her nose.

"What was that about?" She wiped her mouth. "Who is Black Bird?"

"Another ranger. His name's Shawn Baxter." He set his pack in the corner, near a simple folding chair. In the other corner sat two cots, blankets heaped up at the bottom of them and flat pillows at the top.

Noah crossed the room to look through the cabinets lining the opposite wall. He tugged out two large cans—beans of some sort—and then checked down below. "Here we go."

"Anything good?" She offered Boone the thermos.

"Crackers. Baked beans. There's a bag of dried apples if you want to split that with him." He motioned at Boone. "And, of course, more jerky."

Once they'd eaten, Noah unzipped his pack and unloaded the bag with the rest of Boone's wet clothes and several other items. Lucy settled Boone on one of the cots with his toys, then joined Noah near the door.

"Hey, what did you mean out there on the radio? About a fire tower on Lookout Mountain. Oh-900. Are we meeting him tomorrow?"

"It means I want to make sure you two get into the right hands."

"You didn't answer my question."

He sighed. "I want to reach Jasper first and get a second opinion about this. Make sure I'm sending you off with safe people. I...care about you both and don't want anything else bad to happen. You and Boone have been through enough."

A knot of warmth unraveled in her chest, spreading down her arms. *I care about you both.* Noah might be strong-willed and quiet, but he was a man of integrity. She'd been around enough people who weren't, and his quality of character was a marvel to her.

"Don't you trust the other ranger? Shawn?"

"To a point." He stalked over to a box near the rudimentary sink in the kitchenette area. Kneeling, he opened the lid and pulled out shoes. "Hey, look at this. Why don't you try these on."

Lucy followed him, accepting the brown boots. Did Noah think a coworker was involved in this? "Could Shawn send a helicopter here to get us?"

"Not here. That's what I meant about Middle Valley. We'll meet him there tomorrow. It'll give me time to reach Jasper, hopefully." Noah puffed his cheeks up, then blew out a slow breath. "If it had been Derek calling, I wouldn't have hesitated. Or Tim Landry. He's a senior ranger I trust implicitly. Shawn is new to our unit."

"Okay." She nodded slowly. "I appreciate that you're being cautious."

"I also want to reach Jasper's boss, Chief McCoy, and fill him in before I turn you over to authorities." His forehead furrowed. "Wait, you're *okay* about being stuck in the woods one more night?"

"I don't like the woods, but..." She nibbled her lower lip. "I feel safer with you."

Their gazes connected. Noah's hazel eyes were fringed with dark brown lashes and flecked with green. Fine scratches crisscrossed his forehead from when they dove into the bush to hide from the helicopter, and a tiny scar stood out near his left brow. She pointed at it. "What happened here?"

He reached up, felt the nick. "That's from a rock I bumped into when my brother and I were playing hide-and-seek as kids."

"I have a feeling you were excellent at hide-and-seek."

He gave a playful shrug. "I don't want to brag, but one time Jasper and Brielle couldn't find me in the woods for half the day."

Thunder rumbled overhead, interrupting their lighthearted conversation. Lucy looked at the cobwebbed ceiling, then back at the boots.

"I'm glad you told me about Shawn. I won't say anything else if the radio goes off again when you're not there."

"Wait. Anything else? Did you tell Shawn our location on the radio?"

"I don't think so. I said we were with you, and…" Her eyes slammed shut. "I did say you were *in the cabin*. Does that give away where we are?"

"Not necessarily. There are several cabins in the vicinity."

She untied the shoelaces, her stomach just as knotted. "I shouldn't have answered."

"It's alright. You didn't know."

"It's not, though. I might've put us all in danger."

"Hey." He reached out, and she was surprised when he cupped her elbow lightly. "We're both doing the best we can."

He let go, frowning at the boots he'd handed her. "Do those fit?"

"I'll see."

Noah walked over to check on Boone. She unrolled a pair of plaid, threadbare socks Noah had laid out and tugged them on. Then she pulled the boots over them. The footwear was a touch large, but maybe adding a second pair of socks would help.

She ambled around the cabin, ending up at the front window. The hiking boots felt heavy and clunky, but also cozy. Much better than her ankle boots.

She peered out the window. The cloudy glass was cracked in spots, making portions of the landscape blurry and fragmented. Across the clearing, the trees danced in the wind.

Noah joined her a moment later. "Looks like the rain's almost here."

"Good thing we made it."

"Yes. Good thing we made it," he repeated, staring out the window beside her.

They were safe. Fed. Out of the elements.

Then why did her stomach still jump every time she looked into the trees, as though the man after them would burst through at any time?

Noah stretched his arms above his head, then rolled his shoulders. He fought back a yawn. It had to be 2:00 or 3:00 a.m., and the storm system had pummeled the cabin with freezing rain and wind, leaving behind a bitter cold that snuck into the cracks and crevices of the cabin walls.

Would it snow overnight? He'd looked out the window earlier, but the glass was too foggy to see much. Thank the Lord he'd found a raggedy old coat shoved below the box of shoes. Lucy wore it on the cot, and Boone wore Noah's other jacket like a blanket.

He'd dozed off in the chair in the corner for a couple of hours but kept waking up. What had Shawn meant, *Red Knight not available*? Had something happened to Derek? If so, was it tied in with the Harrington murder? And, most importantly, could he trust Shawn Baxter?

On the flip side, why did he think he *couldn't* trust his coworker? Shawn hadn't done anything to warrant Noah's hesitation. It was just…having a history with someone helped to know who they were. And he didn't have a long history with Shawn like he did with Derek. Derek had had his back a couple years ago when two poachers tried to say Noah stole from them and damaged their vehicle. And he'd given Noah time off after Willard Tuttle's murder and his brother Jasper's accident. Other than a tendency toward impatience and micromanagement, Derek was a competent and fair boss.

Noah closed his eyes. He should give Shawn the benefit of the doubt in this situation. Once they had a good night's rest, Noah would lead Lucy and Boone up to the fire watchtower and attempt to rendezvous with Shawn.

A scratching noise came from the front window. His eyes opened. Tree branch rubbing against the glass? No, couldn't be. There weren't any trees directly around the cabin. They'd been cut down to make sure storms didn't blow them onto the structure.

The scratching sounded again, and his muscles tensed. That wasn't natural. It was man-made.

Chills snaked down his spine.

He stood slowly, glancing back at Lucy and Boone. Their combined soft snoring remained steady. It was dark inside the cabin, so no one could see in. Noah pressed up against the wall, inching toward the right front window. Halfway there, he reached down to retrieve his gun from his pack. He gripped it, waiting with bated breath as an alarming realization took his thoughts hostage.

They'd been found.

The crack of breaking glass sent him to the floor. Gunshots. Lucy cried out as the bullet buried itself in the back cabin wall a foot above her head.

"Stay down! Get under the cot."

She launched off the cot, then crawled over to Boone, lifting the crying child and dragging him with her. The blankets covered their combined forms.

"Stay still."

Noah's mind blew through what was happening as he flicked his safety off. Someone just shot through the window. Which meant the person was straight out, near the tree line. The front door had a single lock; it wouldn't hold back a person determined to break in for very long. At least the back door had a double lock and was wedged tightly shut. He'd tried opening it earlier but it hadn't budged. Which meant the killer only had the front windows and door to get inside, and he'd have to get through Noah first.

He scrambled to a better vantage point. Staying low, he tried peering through the window. Line of sight was poor. The darkness hid the shooter.

Another bullet tore through the upper glass panel, inches from his head. He raised his weapon to return fire. Once. Twice.

Boone's and Lucy's quiet sobs carried over as he waited to see if the shooter would engage or move closer and try to get inside the cabin.

Another bullet pierced the window, *thumping* high into the far wall. Lucy gasped as Noah fired two more return shots. If only he could get a better sense of the shooter's location.

He dropped back down and waited. His

muscles constricted painfully. What if he got the back door open and they snuck out that way? The tree line behind the cabin sat only a dozen yards away versus the wide clearing in front of the cabin.

Not ideal. Traveling now, with Boone and Lucy frozen with fright and the weather working against them, would be difficult.

Instead he waited, his jaw taut. Had the shooter given up? Hoped he'd hit the target, then taken off?

Noah carefully positioned himself so he was directly beside the window, able to look out front without putting his face or neck in harm's way.

"Noah, be careful," Lucy whispered.

He motioned for her to stay down as he looked out. Darkness and shadows fell across the field from the trees, but it was impossible to see anything without his flashlight, and that would make him a sitting duck.

He had to wait. Nothing else for it. Several minutes later, he loosened his hold on the weapon, his backbone sagging.

Had the attacker been trailing them? Or had Lucy's accidental admission to Shawn been overheard—or worse, was Shawn working against him? Noah shook his head. He didn't want to believe it. Maybe Shawn's radio call had been intercepted and the criminals after them heard what Lucy said?

"What do we do?" Lucy asked quietly as she soothed Boone's soft cries.

"I'll keep watch. Can you sleep like that on the floor?"

"I'll try. But what if he…"

She cut her words off, but he knew what she was thinking. "I'll stay awake. If he tries to get in, he'll end up with a bullet between the eyes. Once it's daylight, I'll do a full perimeter check before we head out."

She was silent for several seconds. Had she fallen back asleep? "Please be careful, whatever you do."

"I will. Pray that the person is already gone."

Still, if the shooter had been sent here to kill them, he wouldn't go far. He'd be determined to finish the job because there was likely a crime boss breathing down his neck to eliminate the targets.

Boone and Lucy.

They were more than targets to him. Much more. And whoever was trying to kill them would have to go through him first.

SEVEN

Someone was touching her shoulder. Lucy startled awake. Noah kneeled beside her, his features grave. "I'm sorry to wake you, but we need to get moving."

He removed his hand as she rubbed her eyes. Her back ached from sleeping on hard surfaces two nights in a row. A cave floor and the cabin floor. "Did someone really shoot at us last night or was that a bad dream?"

"Unfortunately not a dream."

She sat up, patting down the unruly waves of her hair, then caught Noah watching her.

He stood and transferred his gaze to Boone.

She swallowed the sandpaper dryness

in her throat and peered at Boone, too. He was still asleep, but his legs shifted under the ratty blanket. It had taken a while for him to fall asleep after the awful commotion last night.

"I went out and looked for the shooter an hour ago. Appears I nicked him."

She jerked her head up. "How do you know?"

"I found some bloody leaves on the snow. Wherever he is, he's hurting."

She cringed, then his full statement registered. "There's snow?"

"A light dusting, which worked in our favor. No one is going to stand around all night in that weather. He's gone." Noah looked past her, staring at the wall. Then he leaned forward, his fingers grazing a spot a couple feet over her head.

"Thank the Lord these cots are so low."

She turned, gaping at what he was touching. "Are those…bullet holes?" The second hole sat squarely between her cot and Boone's.

"They are." His mouth set in a grim line.

"We have to get moving. I packed extra food. Keep your coats on. We'll have to eat on the trail."

Fifteen minutes later, she followed him up a winding, snow-covered pathway. In one hand she held crackers and the other clasped Boone's wrist. He had woken up wheezy, so he'd used his inhaler then wolfed down half a roll of crackers and two jerky sticks, drank several large gulps of Noah's filtered water, and now he was spirited and talkative, which served as a useful distraction from the terrifying experience of getting shot at while sleeping.

Noah was exceptionally quiet this morning. Had he slept at all? Guilt clouded her vision as she took in the white-and-brown landscape.

"Have you decided if we'll meet up with your ranger friend?"

"I'm going to try the emergency phone below the fire tower first."

"Who will you call?"

"Jasper." He slowed as the trail peaked

near a ridge, scouting their surroundings. "Then I'll try Derek's cell."

She pursed her lips, her breath clouding in front of her face. Seemed reasonable. The longer they stayed in the woods and dealt with the cold weather and danger-ous man, or men, after her and Boone, the more she was convinced Noah was the only person they could rely on to protect them from this danger.

"So, what's this fire tower like?"

"Tall. Lots of stairs. It's a popular tour-ist spot." He sent her a questioning look. "You've never been there?"

"I've never hiked out here, period. City girl, remember?"

"City girl. Right." He chuckled, but the sound was rougher than the rocky ground. "Care to share what the *human-created issue* was when you went camping?"

She hesitated, letting go of Boone's hand. The child scurried over to Noah. "I've only been camping once, and it didn't go well."

"Did someone in your family get hurt on the trail?"

"No, nothing like that." She dropped her voice so it didn't carry to Boone, now walking a couple feet in front of Noah and kicking clumps of snow. "My parents decided to take us camping one year. But my dad forgot something we needed, tent spikes maybe, and Mom was upset. They ended up arguing nonstop about it."

"That's not a great way to start a vacation."

"That wasn't the worst of it." She pulled a stick off the ground to prod at the snow. "My dad tried to smooth over the situation by taking mom for a hike to see this lake at sunset. But they were so busy fighting they didn't realize they'd gone the wrong way."

"They went off-trail?"

"If that means they got lost in the woods, then yes. Micah and I waited at the campsite all evening." She curled her fingers around the stick until it cracked, then tossed it away from the path. "It was late when they got back, nearly midnight. My mom made us leave, which meant more walking through the woods in the pitch-dark to our car."

"That's a scary situation for a kid to go through. How old were you?"

"Ten." She bit her lip. "The worst part is that day was the catalyst for their separation and divorce. You know, the last nail in the coffin for our family." Her shoulders curled forward.

"That's a bum deal, Lucy. I'm sorry to hear it."

"Thank you. I wish…it had never happened."

His gaze swept the snow-spotted vista. "I get claustrophobic if I'm inside too long. Makes me stir-crazy for the woods. The mountains. Open skies."

"I can tell you're meant to be out here." She straightened. "It makes me extra glad we bumped into you by the river. I don't think we would've lasted long out here without you."

"I don't know, you're pretty tough."

"Oh right, real tough." She flexed her muscles like a bodybuilder, and Noah laughed.

Then he sobered. "By the way, I did think of an alternative plan, in case I... in case we decide not to go with Shawn."

"An alternative plan?" He was including her in decisions, which was what she wanted. But this was tricky. It wasn't just herself they were dealing with. It was a child, a child who might be a key witness in a murder investigation. "What is it?"

"Jasper is coming back from his honeymoon in a couple days. I'm wondering if the best course of action is to get you and Boone to him, so I know without a doubt you're in trustworthy hands."

She nodded slowly, fighting a frown. Why did the thought of being with Jasper, whom she'd never met, open up a black hole in her middle?

Because he wasn't Noah.

Her entire adult life she'd been awkward around men. Unsure of their intent. Skeptical of their motives. But Noah put her at ease just by who he was. She trusted him completely, she realized.

Lucy shook away her strange line of thinking. "Okay. So, we wait for Jasper. What do we do in the meantime?"

"Stay in my territory."

"The woods?" Her stomach pitched low.

"Yes." He watched Boone gather rocks and pile them into a crooked tower. "I can't shake the feeling that there's an ambush waiting for you two when you get back in town. If we find enough food in the hiker's cache at the fire tower, then being out here two more days won't be a problem at all. I can find us shelter until Jasper gets back."

"If you think that's best." She moistened her chapped lips. "I trust you, Noah."

He held her eyes for a long moment then turned and plowed ahead. Lucy called to Boone. As they started back up the trail, Noah's words churned through her mind like the storm last night.

I can't shake the feeling that there's an ambush waiting for you two when you get back in town.

Noah stopped at the edge of the woods on Lookout Mountain. Lucy and Boone stared up at the metal-framed fire tower in the clearing thirty yards ahead. The structure thrust sharply into the sky, and atop the metal base and stairs sat the cab, where forest rangers kept watch for fires in the dry season. Two long windows on each side of the cab gave it an open appearance and 360-degree views.

He'd enjoyed the view from the tower on Lookout Mountain dozens of times while working in this area. Each time he climbed the stairs and took in the wide expanse of Sumter National Forest, it thrilled him.

"That's super-duper tall," Boone said in awe.

Noah smiled. "On a clear day, you can see into North Carolina. That's the next state."

"It looks old." Lucy sank down to retie the laces of her hiking boots.

"It's safe. I've been up there, in the cab part, many times. But we're not going up today."

Boone whined about that, while relief crossed Lucy's face. Her quiet admission earlier interrupted his thoughts. *I trust you, Noah.*

"I wanna go to the top." Boone swung his arms and started forward.

"Hang on, buddy." Noah corralled the child so he didn't step out of their hiding spot.

"Did you see something?" Lucy asked as Boone squirmed between them.

"No, but I'd like you to stay hidden while I get the food."

"Did you hear that, Boone? We have to keep in the woods right now." She addressed Noah. "What time did you tell Shawn we were going to meet him?"

"Nine a.m. My guess is we're about an hour from nine. I'd like to see what happens at nine. Who Shawn brings to meet us. We can watch from the safety of the woods."

Boone sank to his bottom, his curiosity piqued by something on the ground. So far, the vast playground nature provided—sticks, leaves, rocks, animal sightings, moss and now snow—had kept the boy busy and distracted as they alternated hiking and rest.

Noah set his pack down beside Boone's bag, then nudged Lucy. "I'm going to check the ration station first. I want to get there before anyone comes to the area."

"Wouldn't we hear a helicopter coming?"

"Yes, but there's an access road and parking lot about a half mile down Lookout Mountain." It was possible the shooter last night drove in, parked and hiked the reasonable distance to the ranger cabin. "Which is why I want you to stay here while I'm gone."

"We'll stay put, won't we, Boone?"

The child mumbled, flicking leaves off a branch.

"I'm sorry," Lucy whispered to Noah. "He's tired and grumpy." She contemplated the majestic view beyond the trees. "This spot must be beautiful in the fall."

"It is." Noah followed her gaze. "When I come up here, I feel closer to God." He turned to her. "I was wondering, do you have any kind of faith?"

"I did." She sighed. "My parents took us to church. Micah and I went to Sunday school. But that was before..."

"Before your parents separated."

"Yes. And after all the hard stuff that happened, it was difficult to believe in a loving God. Especially when I always felt so alone."

"Understandable." He cleared his throat. "So we're clear. You two stay here. No fire tower. Keep quiet."

"Ten-four." She caught Boone's arms, pulling the child in for an embrace. "We're playing a game of hide-and-seek until Noah gets back, Boone, right?"

"Oh-*kay*." The boy wiggled free.

"See you soon." Noah hefted his pack,

sent Lucy a quick smile, then took off. He hugged the tree line until he reached Lookout Mountain trail, on the opposite side of where Lucy and Boone were hiding. The woods closed in around him, and he tuned his ears to every birdcall, every whisper of the wind, every rustle of leaves.

Lucy's lovely dark eyes filled his mind. Her wounded expression as she shared her family's disastrous camping experience.

How ironic that he'd ended up with a woman who disliked what he loved most. At least he could help her and Boone through this and get them safely into Jasper's hands.

The ration station appeared through the forest. Noah halted, turning to look back up the peak of the fire tower. Unease squeezed his rib cage.

Were Lucy and Boone hiding like he'd told them to?

Leaves crunched nearby, and he whipped around. A squirrel clung upside down to a tree, chirping angrily. He whistled at it, then continued on to the ration station, his boots crunching the snow.

Several feet from the station, Noah froze. In front of the telephone booth–sized wooden structure that housed food, large footprints marred the fresh snow. A hiker must've been here earlier. Or a bear? His muscles turned to stone as he leaned over and inspected the marks. No claw marks. Symmetrical. But how had he not heard or seen any other sign of them on the way over to the ration station? Unless they came in from the west.

Noah lifted the heavy latched lid of the wooden box and peered inside. Empty. How could that be? The number of hikers dwindled during the winter months, and normally these stations stayed well stocked in December and January for that very reason. He checked below and behind the storage container.

"We ate it all."

Noah snatched a rock from the ground and whipped around at the male voice behind him. A balding, stocky man stood a dozen feet away, a rifle aimed at Noah's chest. The man who attacked Boone and Lucy near the waterfall and cave. A white gauzy bandage wrapped his shoulder. *The shooter.*

"You again." Noah held the rock out of sight. "What do you want?"

"You're going to pay for shooting me."

"You shot at us first." If he asked the man questions maybe he could distract him. "Why're you going after them?"

"The kid has somethin' we want."

"What could a child have that you'd want so bad?"

The man glanced at the sky, a deep laugh springing from his belly. "That's none of—"

Noah threw the rock at the gunman's head. It struck his left shoulder, and he cried out in surprise and pain. Noah lunged at him, landing a jab on the man's cheek. He howled and reeled backward.

The butt of a black rifle came out of nowhere, connecting with Noah's forehead in a hard blow. He buckled to his knees, stars dancing in his peripheral.

"Bad move, Mountain Man." A shadow fell over Noah as a second person appeared. He attempted to roll away, but the two men shoved him down then hedged him in with their legs. Noah tried to disentangle himself, but his body wouldn't respond.

No. Lucy and Boone sat alone up there. Unprotected. Lost without his help. She'd trusted him, and he'd failed her.

"Leave him for dead."

The thick end of the rifle flew at his face again, and pain exploded behind his eyes.

Everything went dark.

EIGHT

"Can we climb the tower now?"

Lucy released her hair from the tight bun and finger-combed the strands, flinching at the snarls and knots. "Not yet. Mr. Noah just left. He told us to stay here." Boone's green-and-blue bag caught her eye. "You want to play with your little dog, Mr. Barkey?"

"Yeah, okay."

She grabbed the bag and retrieved the white plastic toy. Boone reached for it, hugging it to him. He set Mr. Barkey on the ground and spoke in little boy whispers, pretending to have a conversation with the toy.

"Can I make him talk so I can hear

Sammy?" A hopeful expression covered his sweet face.

Maybe that wasn't the best suggestion after all. "How about you do the talking? Sammy can bark later."

Boone's face fell. He sighed theatrically and set the dog near her legs.

"Mr. Barkey is tired and he needs a nap."

"Should I rub his back to put him to sleep, too?" She grasped the toy and smiled at Boone. Her fingertip brushed a button on the bottom, and the sound of a barking dog rang out.

"It's Sammy!" Boone screeched with happiness.

"Whoops. Shh." She turned it off then thrust the toy dog back in the bag. "I did that on accident. Let's keep quiet for now." Making that much noise was the opposite of what Noah asked them to do.

Boone stood, swinging his arms. He shoved the toe of one shoe in the snow, rustling the sticks and leaves beneath. Then he kicked out, sending some of the dirt and snow onto his bag. Clearly, he was upset.

"Boone. That's enough."

"I want to go on the big tower."

She knew children. Knew the signs of a tired child. Knew that his lack of sleep the last two nights lessened his ability to cope. "Boone. Look at me. We have to wait for Mr. Noah."

Boone's eyes welled up, and Lucy almost gave in. But no, they couldn't do what Noah had told them not to. "I'm sorry, we have to wait a little while longer."

"I don't wanna wait!" he wailed.

She touched his arm, placating him, but Boone twisted away and took off past the bushes. Darting out of the woods and into the clearing, the child beelined for the fire tower.

Oh, no. "Boone!" Lucy called, frighteningly aware how her voice must be carrying across the mountaintop. She ran after him. "Come back!"

Boone reached the tower and mounted

the stairs like a rabbit chased by a coyote. He was halfway up the structure before she even got to the base. Her pulse pounded in her ears as she raced up to the second level. The structure was high, and its position at the top of the mountain made it seem even higher. Her legs shook with each stride.

"Boone, stop!" He'd been through a lot the last few days, but this outburst could put them all in danger. "It's not safe up here."

Her breaths were roaring in and out when she caught him on the top level. The cab, Noah called it. They stood on the metal grating, Lucy holding his wrists a few feet from the door. White-crested mountains folded gently all around them. Like Noah said, the fire tower's view was spectacular.

But she was too irritated with Boone to enjoy it. "You can't run off like that, Boone."

"I just wanted to see it up here." He hung his head. "Please?"

"There are dangerous people looking for us." She craned her neck to check out the door leading into the cab. "We can look inside for one minute, then we have to get back to the ground."

She led him to the door. The knob turned easily, then they stepped inside. A long arm snaked out, wrapping around her chest and shoulders.

Lucy screamed.

The man's forearm squeezed her throat, cutting off her cry for help. *Noah.* Had he heard them?

Boone shouted from across the room. "Ms. Lucy! No. There's a gun!"

A cold, hard weight pressed on her temple. Lucy fought off a burst of adrenaline that scorched her skin. She had to be strong for Boone.

Pain shimmied down her arms from his rough grip. "Take me, and leave him."

"Oh no, lady. We want the kid."

"He doesn't know anything. Leave him alone!"

"I think he does. I think he's got something we want." He leaned in, his rancid breath blowing over her cheek. "You're coming with us, too."

"He's a child. He doesn't know what happened. Let him go!" She struggled against the man, then suddenly he threw her toward Boone.

She landed with a painful thud, elbow smacking into the window above the child. Lucy cried out, then reached for Boone, bringing him into her arms. How could they get away? The man stood directly beside the doorway, blocking the only way off the tower.

Had Noah heard her calling Boone a minute ago?

She caught the blond man's sneering gaze. "We have nothing. It all went underwater in the river." What did they want from him?

The man laughed, the sound like rocks crashing together. "I see you looking for that big guy. He won't hear you, sweetheart. We already got him."

We? Had they ambushed Noah near the

ration station? Her heart turned over in her chest, and her vision blurred.

Was Noah dead?

A sharp stick was poking Noah's cheek. He moved his head, blinking through the intense fog that kept his brain from working. Where was he? He struggled upright, his hands grasping the snow and dirt. His ear felt numb, and his brain pounded at the movement. Where—

The fire tower. Lookout Mountain. Lucy. Boone. Where were they?

He rubbed his eyes. The light blinded him, and he squinted. From what he could tell, the sun was at its peak in the sky. Could it be almost noon?

But that meant...

His erratic pulse kicked in as he tried to stand. Liquid trickled down his temple, and he swayed, landing on his knees again.

He touched the spot. Dry, sticky blood coated his fingertips, and black dots edged his vision. Noah closed his eyes, inhaling slow, deep breaths. After a few moments, he opened them and felt for his gun. Gone. Then he reached back for his pack. Nothing. The backpack was missing. His rations, CB radio and even his truck keys. *No.* Had his attackers taken it?

What happened to Lucy and Boone?

He struggled to his feet. The world tilted sideways, and he leaned into a tree trunk and closed his eyes until the dizziness passed. Once it did, he scoured the area, looking for any sign of his gray pack on the snowy ground. Nothing. They'd taken all his supplies.

The fire tower stood like a silent sentinel on the mountaintop.

"Lucy!" he shouted. No answer. *God, please keep them safe.*

Noah followed the path as quickly as he could put one foot in front of the other.

At the top he slowed, searching for the spot where he'd last seen them. There, beneath a pair of loblolly pines near the crown. He rushed over. The snowy ground was trampled, leaves and twigs gathered in Boone-created piles.

"Lucy?" His chest caved in. No sign of them.

Boone's green-and-blue bag caught his eye, tucked under a heap of leaves. Had someone been planted near the tower, and the men had gotten Lucy and Boone?

Shawn. Was his coworker the mole in the gun smuggling ring?

Ice water poured through his veins. He stood, shouldering the child's bag, then hurtled up the clearing to the base of the tower. Memory clicked in. There was a second pathway to this tower via the park service road. It was hidden and narrow, used by rangers if the normal pathway was jammed with tourists. The men must've come up that way.

Sweat stung his eyes as he lit up the stairs. Atop the forty-foot tower, he advanced with cautious steps. What if it was a trap?

He grabbed the doorknob and rammed through shoulder-first, then twisted to look behind the door. The large space, filled with two sets of chairs near the front window and a small trash can, sat empty.

"No." He released a hard breath.

Noah dashed outside. The sunlight blinded him as he considered his next steps. At least two to three hours had passed since he was knocked out and Lucy and Boone were abducted. Which meant the men who took them were long gone.

A bible verse he'd memorized as a child grounded his scattered thoughts now.

"But they that wait upon the Lord shall renew their strength; they shall mount up with wings as eagles; they shall run, and not be weary; and they shall walk, and not faint."

"Renew my strength, Lord. Help me find them. Please."

The emergency phone at the ranger shed. It was down the mountain, near the parking lot. The place he'd intended to check after they left the ration station.

Noah secured Boone's bag and raced down the stairs. His head pounded with each slap of his boot on metal. He gritted his teeth and pushed through the pain. At the bottom of the tower, he circled the concrete pad and canvassed the ground. Some of the snow had melted, making the earth ripe for tracking. No one knew this section of Sumter like he did.

Near the second path, dozens of crushed twigs gave away the kidnappers' direction. As he figured, the men had taken the service road, allowing them the shortest route uphill and the quickest way to their car. Noah took off downhill. Dodging branches and weaving around rocks, he ran most of the way down the path, head pounding like a drum. About a hundred yards out from the service parking lot, he slowed, cutting into the tree line. Edging quietly forward, he came upon the parking lot.

It was empty. Too bad his truck wasn't parked here. Not that it would help, without his keys. Beside the small parking area, which fit only five to six cars, sat a large gray shed used by rangers. Canoes, emergency kits, extra supplies and myriad other items were stored inside.

Noah wiped his brow. No vehicles. Which meant Lucy and Boone were gone. Taken by men who'd been shooting at them for over twenty-four hours. Did that mean— Could they be...?

No. He refused to let the thought take root.

He would find them.

Noah straightened. Did the shed still have the spare ATVs for emergencies? If so, maybe there was a chance of catching up. He slunk through the woods, his movements cautious as he approached the clearing with the shed.

A blue jay cawed a warning from a nearby branch.

He jogged closer, looking for tire tracks. They were easy to find. He followed the tracks for several yards. From the tread marks, it appeared they'd been taken in a large vehicle. A van?

The first thing to do was call his brother. Noah tried the shed door and found it locked. He circled the building, then jarred open a back window and climbed through. Once inside, he located the old, corded phone on the wall and dialed Jasper's cell.

His brother answered on the fourth ring. "Jasper Holt. Who is this?"

"Jas, I'm in trouble."

"Noah. What is going on? Chief McCoy called, asked if I'd heard from you. Where are you? Aren't you supposed to be on the AT in Virginia?"

"Plans changed. I'm still here. In Sumter." Hiking, but definitely *not* alone. *Not* relaxing.

"Details."

Noah ran through the first night, when he found Lucy's car on the river, then Boone and his asthma issues and retrieving the inhaler. He mentioned the attack near the waterfall, spending the night in the cave, what happened last night at the cabin and the fact that he believed Shawn

Baxter was part of this. Last he shared what happened near the fire tower.

"You're telling me you've been shot at *three* times and beat up?"

"Yeah, and I have the head wound to prove it." He barely believed it himself.

"But you're okay?"

"I am, but Lucy and Boone aren't."

Jasper made a frustrated sound. "The young woman, who is she again?"

"Lucy is Boone's social worker. She has temporary custody until the judge assigns PG to Boone's closest relative."

"Boone Harrington." Jasper blew a hard breath, creating static on the line. "Poor kid. I hope his mom makes it."

"Me, too. Reminds me, one of the perps who came after me acted like Boone has something they want. I'm trying to figure out what."

"You said the men have Lucy and Boone?"

Noah closed his eyes. "Yeah. Just got to them a couple hours ago."

"Man. This is not good."

"No, none of it is." Noah could picture his older brother, a fist pressed to his mouth.

"You've called Tunnel Creek PD, right?"

"No. I haven't been able to reach anyone except Shawn. I lost my cell when the man attacked them the first night. And my radio wasn't working until we reached the ranger cabin last night."

"The storm, maybe?"

"That's what I thought about the radio reception, too. What was strange is Shawn said Derek wasn't available. I don't know what that means. I wonder if Derek discovered something and was..." Noah swallowed. "Taken out?"

Jasper whistled again. A feminine voice sounded in the background on his brother's end. Kinsley, Noah's new sister-in-law. Jasper spoke away from the phone for a moment, then addressed Noah. "You said you're at the ranger shed at the base of Lookout Mountain?"

"Yes." His leg muscles bunched, and he paced as far as the phone cord would let him. Jasper could advise Noah on his next course of action, but he couldn't do anything else from his hotel room. Noah scrubbed his face. "I'm trying to figure out where the men would take them. I need to get to them."

"My guess is they wouldn't risk taking them into town…" Jasper muttered, deep in thought. "Or take them far away, because then there's a risk of being seen once we put an APB out. So…"

"So, where's a building or structure in the forest that's under the radar…"

"Hey! What about the old water treatment facility off thirty-six? It's closed, but we've had to chase teenagers out of it. That's what, three or four miles from the fire tower?"

Noah's eyes widened. The large industrial building had been shut down a decade ago, but it was still standing and completely hidden from the main road.

"Jasper, I think you're onto something. How about some prayer that I get there in time."

"You got it. Hey, once you find them, go

to our cabin. Security system works. You can call McCoy with my work cell. He'll make sure they stay safe."

"Stay safe?" Kinsley, Jasper's new wife, came on the line. "Noah, are you okay?"

Noah had been skeptical of Jasper and Kinsley's relationship when she returned to Tunnel Creek, especially because she'd broken Jasper's heart in high school. But after she helped save Jasper during the gun smuggling incident last year, he'd become convinced of her love for his brother.

"Not really, sis." She'd said to call her that when they got engaged months ago. It felt weird at first, but he'd gotten used to it. Kinsley was an only child, and her parents had been killed in a car accident a decade ago in Tunnel Creek. Noah and Jasper, Jasper's son, Gabe, their sister, Brielle, and their mom had become Kinsley's family.

"What's going on?"

"Ah, just some crazy stuff at work." *A killer chasing us through the forest. Gun-*

fire. Kidnapping. Stuff that is not in the ranger's training manual.

Jasper's voice came back over the line. "Noah, do what I told you to. My place. Got it? I'll be home ASAP."

"I'm glad to hear it."

They ended the call. Noah pulled a tarp off an older model four-wheeler then checked the gas. Good to go. Five minutes later, he emerged from the shed, muttering and pushing the ATV. Boone's bag was slung over his back, inhaler and toys zipped up inside. He wanted to have something familiar for the poor kid. Boone had been through so much.

Noah glanced at the sky. He missed his watch. Of all the times he could've left it at home...

Already the sunlight had changed. Muted. It was past the middle of the day. Ever since the time change a few weeks back, night swooped in like a hawk after its prey. Soon the shadows of evening would take over the forest and that worried him.

While he was comfortable in the dark in the woods, riding a noisy ATV with headlights—dim as they might be—could give away his position.

He tried starting the ATV. A tiny rumble growled in the engine. He revved it again, and this time the machine sputtered to life. Noah pumped his fist in the air, then slung his leg over and set off. He followed the tire tracks until the access road hit a bypass road, then concrete took over. He rode along the shoulder, his mind racing in a thousand directions but always landing on the same plea.

Please, God, let them be at the water treatment plant. Help me find them.

Several minutes later, he steered the agile machine off the shoulder, down an incline and deep into the forest. He was about a half mile from the plant now, and he couldn't risk being heard. After maneuvering the four-wheeler into a huge thicket, he killed the ignition, secured Boone's bag inside the front trunk com-partment, tucked the key deep in his pocket and set off toward the facility.

Would he make it in time?

partment, tucked the key deep in his
pocket and set off toward the facility.
Would he make it in time?

NINE

Lucy's spine rubbed against a concrete
wall. A blindfold covered her eyes and
the top part of her nose, and her wrists
were bound behind her back. The over-
powering scent of body odor and mold
stung her nose, and the *drip-drip* of water
scalded her ears. Cold concrete sent trem-
ors over her arms and legs. Boone's small
body pressed into hers, the only light in
the darkness.

"I'm scared."

"It's okay. I'm here with you." She
swallowed gingerly, her throat raw from
screaming at the fire tower. "God is, too.
He won't leave us."

It felt strange saying that out loud since
she'd been denying that very truth for her

entire adult life. But for some reason, in that cold, echoey room, she was certain it was the truth.

"Can God get us away from this bad place?"

"I think so. Let's pray that He does." She rested her chin on the top of his head. "Please, God, we need Your help. Show us a way out of here. Keep us safe. Amen."

"Amen."

Her mind went straight to Noah. Was he alive? Tears formed, but instead of falling down her cheeks, they soaked into the blindfold.

"I'm sorry I went to the top part."

"It's okay, Boone. It's hard to wait sometimes."

"Why do you have a shirt on your eyes?"

Lucy straightened. "You don't have a blindfold on your face?"

"Kinda. Mine fell on my chin." He spit like there was disgusting food in his mouth.

She angled her face to try and see from under the foul-smelling piece of cloth.

"Can you see where we are?" Relying on his five-year-old eyes and understanding would be difficult, but at least they could try.

"I dunno this place. It's big and dark and there's no couch."

No couch. Of course not, because it felt like a factory or facility. She replayed the last few hours. The men had dragged them down the mountain and put them into a large vehicle. From what she'd seen before they blindfolded her, it appeared to be a white cargo van. She'd listened intently to their conversation. Shadow Back Mountain was the only location name she could remember.

They'd driven for several minutes over winding, paved roads. No other traffic had passed by. She'd listened intently for that. Which meant they must still be in the forest.

Something solid but small fell in her lap. Little fingers tickled her legs. Boone's hands? "Your hands are tied in front of you?" This could definitely work in their favor.

Footsteps snapped her attention to the far end of the room. It took the person nearly ten seconds to reach them, which meant it was a large room.

"Quit talking."

Recognition stunned her. That voice belonged to the burly man who'd attacked them near the waterfall. She was sure of it. And he'd been there at the fire tower, near the bottom. So far it was the burly short man and the thin blond man who'd grabbed them atop the fire tower.

She gulped down a sob. Was Noah okay?

"Where are we?" she demanded.

"Look, lady, you aren't asking questions. *I* am."

Another person approached, this time with faster footsteps. Lighter. The blond man? He'd seemed nervous and agitated up on the fire tower.

"You're not supposed to be talking

to them." The blond man had a higher-pitched, nasal voice.

"I was just seeing if they were still here and telling them to be quiet."

"They're not going anywhere, you idiot. The Big Man is going to talk to the kid before we take them to the mine."

A mine?

"I don't know why he thinks the kid knows where it is. He's like three."

"I'm five!" Boone interjected.

"Please," she pleaded. "He's a child. He doesn't know what happened that night."

"We'll let the Big Man sort it out. Then we're done with you both," the burly man snorted.

She ground her teeth. "You're bullies, picking on a little boy like this. He doesn't know anything."

"Then you better hope you do," the blond man mocked her. "Otherwise, this is going to be over nice and quick."

"Stop speaking like that around him."

"Tell you what." One of them stalked over. She kicked out at him, and the man growled, then let out an oath. Two sweaty hands grabbed her shoulders, yanking her upright. Pain exploded in her arms. "You can just go sit by yourself."

Boone called her name, and she jerked in the man's tight grasp.

"It's okay, buddy. I won't be far." She addressed the burly man as he dragged her away. "You can do the right thing and let us go. The boy doesn't know what's going on."

"You just can't shut your mouth, can you?" he snarled, pushing her forward.

Boone called for her again.

"Hey, buddy, where are you?"

"Buddy? That's the kid's name? I thought it was Boone?"

Lucy answered quickly in case Boone was nearby and corrected her. "His name is Ben, but I call him Buddy." Maybe she could confuse them. Make them think they had the wrong child.

"Ben? What?" The burly man stopped short. "Hey, get over here!"

Footsteps pounded the floor as the second man rushed over. "What now?"

She turned her face toward the man holding her hostage. "His name is Ben. Weren't you looking for a child with a different name?"

"Lady, you're a liar," the taller, blond man ground out. "I heard her say Boone when we were at that big tower place. She's lying. Don't—"

"You misheard me, then," Lucy cut in. "His name is Ben. You have to let him go."

"Wait, is she playing us?"

"Yeah, she is." The burly man shook the back of her shirt like she was a kitten and he held it by the scruff. "Can't you tell?"

They argued back and forth, their harsh language making her shudder. Hopefully Boone couldn't hear it. "Nice try, lady. For a looker, you're pretty dumb. Neither of you is leaving here."

He shoved her down against another wall. Pain zinged down her spine as she bumped into the unforgiving surface.

The men walked away, leaving her alone in silence. A box of some sort jutted out next to her, a few inches long and a couple inches wide. Slightly larger than a cell phone. Was it an outlet of some sort?

Where was Boone? "Buddy?" she called out. "Can you hear me?"

No answer.

Lucy choked down despair. Her arms and legs felt like blocks of ice. What had she done? Now she and Boone were separated, and Noah was probably dead. Even her lie to the men about Boone's identity hadn't worked. Her heart throbbed as childhood memories returned like a ruthless deluge of rain. Noah had called her brave. Instead, she felt weak. Powerless. Like everything she touched fell apart. Her family. Her relationships. The people she cared about. Noah's kind, strong profile lit up her mind. He might even be dead, because of her.

She tipped her head against the concrete wall as tears cascaded down her cheeks like the waterfall they'd hid under two days ago.

Please, God. I have nothing. I need You.

The growl of a far-away voice drew Lucy awake. She blinked and shook her head. How long had she been asleep? She straightened, her back bumping the wall. She was still tied up. Still stuck. Still alone. Her words to Boone earlier came back to haunt her. *God is with us.*

"God. If You're there, please help. I don't know what to do."

Where was Boone?

She rubbed the thin rope around her wrists into the rectangular outlet she'd noticed earlier. The edges weren't sharp, but they were defined. Maybe extra friction would do the trick. As she rubbed, she nodded roughly, trying to loosen the blindfold. It un-bunched and fell lower, covering her nose. She could make out faint light through the thin fabric now. After several seconds of rough friction, the wrist rope had loosened enough that it was no longer cutting into her skin.

How much longer did they have?

"Boone?" She kept her voice low.

No answer. The blindfold slipped down more. Shadows marked the edges of the room. Fear crept up her limbs. Gray evening light seeped in through the high windows. Was it that late already? The men said the *Big Man* was coming tonight. What did the men want with Boone? Were they just going to interrogate him, then—

The sound of cracking glass burst from somewhere above her head. She rolled away from the wall so the sharp bits didn't fall on her. The rope on her wrists and ankles loosened but didn't release, which made the movement awkward. She hobbled to her knees, then to her feet, wobbling until she gained enough balance to stay upright.

"Hello? Is someone there?"

The blindfold sank below her nose, covering her mouth and chin instead. At last, she could see. She could make out massive columns in the long room. Huge tanks sat at the far end, stairs leading up

to them. What was this place? She scrutinized the walls. A dozen high, rectangular
windows lined the room. But the outside
of each window appeared to be partially
shielded by bushes and trees and...earth.
The ground. Were they being kept in a
basement?

"Boone?" she called again, this time
louder. "Are you here?"

Another cracking sound burned her
ears, and she turned toward the window.
Who was there?

Noah set the wrench aside, then pulled
the pieces of glass carefully from the window. The water treatment facility was
surrounded by overgrown hedges on all
sides. He'd snuck onto the premises easily enough, but two men patrolled the
actual building, and he'd been forced to
duck behind the bushes for longer than
he'd wanted.

He frowned. He'd found Boone first,
held in a smaller section of the facility
on the east side. But no Lucy. Noah hadn't

wanted to leave Boone behind the massive sweet gum just inside the tree line, but the boy seemed to understand the need to stay still and quiet.

Finally, Noah found Lucy near the front of the facility. A dangerous location.

Noah picked away the last large piece of glass. "Lucy?"

"Noah? Where are you?" Her voice quivered like she'd been crying.

"I'm here. Look up."

"You're here." She sniffled. Definitely crying.

"Are you alone?"

"Yes! I don't know where Boone is. They separated us."

"I got him already." He pushed himself through the opening feetfirst. The floor was a solid eight- to ten-foot drop, and he held the edge of the window, then landed with a hard *thud*. When he straightened, she launched at him. He wrapped his arms around her.

"You're alive!" Her face pressed into his chest. "My wrists are tied."

"Are you hurt?" He let go and turned her around to untie her. "Did they...?"

"No one touched me other than to tie me up and yell when I tried to ask questions. Then they dragged me in here." She shook her arms out.

"We need to get you out of here."

"Yes. The two men talked about someone coming tonight. The *Big Man*, they said."

He scowled. Shawn Baxter, he'd guess. As much as he wanted to find out the person's identity, they needed to disappear. "Let me find something to climb on."

A cluster of empty shelves were piled against the corner several feet away. He rushed over, grabbing one and lugging it toward the broken window. Then another. Lucy joined him, and they finished with three, stacked back to front. Should be tall enough.

"You first. Be careful. Men are patrolling the yard around the building. If they're nearby, climb behind the bushes and don't make a sound."

She nodded, then clambered onto his threaded fingers. The shelves groaned under her weight and the movement. How would he climb out if the shelves barely supported her?

"Hold on to the windowsill. Watch out for the glass."

He held his breath and pushed on the bottom of her boots as she reached the narrow windowsill then drew herself up to the broken window. She slipped through headfirst, and he released the breath as her boots finally slid through. She was out. Thank the Lord.

The unmistakable sound of a car door slamming outside sent Noah's pulse into a sprint. He had to get out. Now.

He leaped on the upended bookshelves, grimacing as the wood cracked beneath him. With one massive effort, he pushed off, leaping at the windowsill. He gripped the edge, muscling his way higher, slithering through the opening.

Pain pricked his skin as pieces of glass left in the window frame scraped his face.

He inched away from the sharp edge, and flailed his feet for a foothold or an extra push off the wall inside.

Lucy grabbed his arms and helped pull, her mouth pinched with effort. It felt like it took an hour to pass through the broken window. Finally, his legs cleared it, then his boots. He fell in between the bushes and the building, his chest heaving.

She jerked her head around at another noise. "Was that a car door?"

"Think so." Noah held his crouching position, peering through the thick, prickly bushes to the front of the water treatment plant. "Once they go inside, we make a run for it."

A white van sat in the parking lot and, beside it, a black truck. A jolt of familiarity struck him. Was that Shawn's truck?

She looked around wildly. "Where is Boone?"

"He's back there, in the woods." He pointed toward the trees behind the building. "C'mon."

They stood. He linked their hands, then

they burst from the bushes and sprinted across the yard toward Boone. A shout sounded behind them. *They'd been spotted.*

"Hurry." Noah urged her faster. "Go right! He's over there."

"Ms. Lucy!"

Boone's voice. Lucy veered toward the child.

Then a *ping-ping* rang out. Shots. Lucy screamed and flung herself toward the cover of the woods and Boone. Noah followed, lifting the child and tucking him against his chest. He pushed Lucy deeper into the forest, until colder air enveloped them. The deadly *whop* of a bullet hitting a tree trunk to his left set his feet on fire.

"Keep moving!"

Every few seconds he'd call out directions. Branches whipped his forehead and neck, and his head pounded from the knock to it earlier. Lucy panted beside him, her gate uneven from the heavy hiking boots. They ran for three or four minutes, Boone clasped in his arms. He guided them toward the rise, where the ATV lay hidden in a cluster of bushes just beyond the ridgeline.

"Almost there." They crested the hill, and he pointed. "I found a ride for us. It's back there." He pushed through the underbrush to reach the small all-terrain vehicle.

"Can we all fit on that?" she panted.

"We're going to try." He placed the child down, and his gaze connected to Lucy's. "Pray this thing starts. I had a tough time getting it going earlier."

A man's shout carried through the forest.

"They're closing in." Noah jumped on first, then Boone in the middle, then Lucy. He grasped the handlebars and revved the engine. "Hold on tight."

He gunned the throttle, and they launched forward.

The forest swallowed them as he drove away. Cold air bit into his face and stung his eyes. Without goggles, he had to squint to see. He glanced behind them every minute or so. Soon it would be pitch-dark. He had no idea how much gas was left in the ATV, or what lengths the men would go to in order to find them. Right now, they needed to put major distance between themselves and the water treatment facility. Get to Jasper and Kinsley's cabin and hole up. Find out what Lucy had heard in that basement.

Figure out who this *Big Man* was before anyone else got killed.

He had a strong feeling he knew who it was already. Noah pictured Shawn Baxter, and his shoulders stiffened. How long had the other ranger been involved in this?

A thought struck Noah like an uppercut.

Did Shawn have something to do with the expired EpiPen in his safety kit?

TEN

Noah drove the four-wheeler over the dark, snowy forest floor. Moonlight guided him toward Jasper's cabin. They'd gone maybe one and a half or two miles, and he could tell by Boone's squirming the boy was as ready to get off this thing as Noah was. His backside was sore, but they couldn't stop. Not yet. The thought of getting cleaned up and changing his clothes—and food, lots of food—at Jasper's place was a tantalizing incentive to keep going.

He'd distanced them from the road, keeping among the trees. They'd crossed one creek and had another up ahead. He had to jump off to test the water's depth. That plus the darkness made it slow going.

He was about 90 percent certain they were headed in the right direction—and 10 percent terrified they weren't.

On the other side of the second creek, the off-road vehicle sputtered, then stalled.

Noah groaned. "Sounds like we're out of gas."

They climbed off, moving stiffly after sitting for so long. Could the creek they'd just crossed be Bear Claw Creek? That led to Bear Claw Pond, which lay downhill from Jasper's place.

"Do you know where we are?" Lucy asked.

"I think so. My brother's place isn't far from here." He helped Boone onto his back in a piggyback position. The child's movements were slow, and his breathing had the telltale crackling, wheezing sound. "It should only be about a half-hour hike this way."

"Noah." She came up beside him and touched his arm. "We don't have Boone's bag."

"I got it." He pulled open the front com-partment of the four-wheeler, retrieving the green-and-blue bag. "I found it when I was searching for you two by the fire tower."

"Thank the Lord." She shuddered with relief.

He cocked his head. "Sounds like you've been praying?"

Her soft smile snatched his breath. "Yeah, I did. A lot, actually. For you, for us." She tucked her chin, breaking the eye contact, then pointed at Boone. "He should probably use his inhaler now." She stared at him. "Wait, where's your pack?"

"The perps got it. My weapon, all my gear."

"Noah, I'm sorry." She looked like she wanted to say something else, then stopped. "I'm so glad you're okay."

"Me, too." He rubbed his temple and worked up a half smile. "Maybe they finally knocked some sense into me."

"You have a lot more sense than most men I've met."

He blinked at her compliment, then handed her Boone's bag. "Here."

Lucy found his inhaler and helped Boone take two puffs. The medicine worked immediately, loosening the crackling noise coming with each breath. He readjusted the child's position on his back, and Boone laid his head against Noah's upper shoulder. The trusting gesture sent a shot of warmth through him, and when he made eye contact with Lucy, she watched them with a shuttered expression. What would this be like under better circumstances, offering his own child a piggyback like his dad had when Noah was young?

"He really likes you."

"The feeling's mutual." Noah paused. "I lost my dad when I was a kid, too. Leaves a big hole in your heart. I feel for him."

Her eyes widened. "Oh, Noah. You did? I'm so sorry."

"Thanks. It's okay. It was a long time ago."

"That doesn't matter. It's still painful to lose a parent at any age."

"True. I guess there are different ways to lose them, too." He cleared his throat. "You ready?"

Lucy nodded, and he turned and set off. She struggled to stay close by, and Noah slowed his pace. As he headed up the next rise, the weight on his back turned limp, and he held on tighter to Boone's arms. Poor little guy was wiped.

His mind reversed to their kidnappers at the water treatment plant. "Did you overhear anything else back there? Any names or plans, dates or locations?"

"No names. Just the one who said the *Big Man* was coming tonight. Like he was the man in charge."

Noah's boot snapped a stick. "I'm pretty sure it's Shawn."

"That's terrible if it's true."

"I know. Can't believe it. What about physical descriptions of the men?"

"There's a tall, thin blond man and the shorter, heavier one you fought with in the forest." She was silent for several moments as they struggled uphill.

"Oh! The men mentioned a mine."

A mine? He halted midstride. "The only mine around here is at Shadow Back Mountain. There's a mine and sightseeing tours, with an old village in the valley below. Have you been there?"

"No, I haven't." She leaned over, and their constant, clouded breaths mingled. "They also acted like Boone has something they want. They said the Big Man was going to ask him about it."

"I got the same impression when they ambushed me at the food cache." He dashed sweat from his forehead. "What would a child have that they'd want? They think he overheard plans or names, maybe?"

"It sounded like they think Boone took a physical item from his house."

"What, like evidence?"

"I don't know." She straightened. "But they seemed desperate to find it."

They set off again, his thoughts in turmoil. Why would the men set up camp at the mine? Last he checked, the mine and historic village were closed for repairs and updates. Noah turned east as they crested another small hill. "What if there's something else in his bag?"

"I don't think so. We saw all the items inside." She was silent for a few seconds. "I guess we can check at the cabin and see."

"Speaking of." Noah slowed, pointing. "Look at that."

Through the trees, Jasper and Kinsley's cabin shone in a colorful display of holiday spirit. White lights lined the roof, and icicle lights dangled from the edges. The windows were encircled with colored lights, making the building a Christmas night-light in the forest. Huge bulbs hung from an oak tree in the backyard, and tiny electric candles shone from the windows.

"It's beautiful," Lucy exclaimed. "Like out of a fairy tale."

"What is that?" Boone asked in a drowsy voice. "Christmas lights!"

"That's my brother's cabin. Wait till you see the front and the inside. Boone, you get to sleep in a real bed tonight. And eat real food."

"Mhm." Boone's happy murmur made Noah smile. He turned to meet Lucy's gaze and found her grinning, too.

"So, you live here?" Lucy asked as they climbed the last hill.

"I do. There are housing options for rangers, cabins and bunkhouses, but I'd rather be near my family. It's close enough to work and I can help my mom and Jasper out when they need it."

"And your mom lives here, too?"

"She does. There are four bedrooms and a den on the first floor. Three bathrooms. Mom moved in a couple years ago when Jasper's ex-wife passed away. The living arrangement worked out for all of us. Mom helped with Gabe, and she cooked for Jasper and me and did laundry. Can't complain, you know?" He paused, his chest heaving from the inclined hike and extra weight. "Now that Jasper's married, I'll have to figure something else out.

Mom will stay for a little while, until she can find a place in Tunnel Creek."

"Brielle lives somewhere else?"

"Right. She lives on the other side of Tunnel Creek. Near her antique store."

"Do you wish she lived here, too?"

"I don't know. Might be a bit much if we were all in the cabin. We'd just like to see her more often. But she's passionate about her business, and it's booming. She's a very independent woman, kind of like someone else I know." He nudged her with his elbow.

"But she has such a wonderful family. If I did…"

"If you did…" Noah prompted, his brows drawing together.

"I would want to be around them all the time."

Noah chuckled. "I love my family, but even I don't want to be around them *all* the time."

They reached the top, and Noah paused to catch his breath. Lucy did the same, setting her hands on her knees and bending forward.

"I feel like I'm at a hiking boot camp. A weeklong one." She huffed, pointing at something up ahead. "There's another building. Is that a garage?"

"That's the original cabin. Built in 1928. Now it's my mom's art studio."

"She's an artist?"

"She is. Mixed media. Acrylic. Pottery. If it's messy, she's right there in the middle of it." Noah led them toward the front porch, then set Boone down on the steps. The child gazed in wonder at the twinkling icicle lights above his head. "I'm going to check the perimeter of the place, make sure everything looks alright. I'll be right back."

Noah strode around the cabin, checking windows and locks and looking for anything unusual. Normally there were four dogs here to keep watch, but his mom had taken Gabe and three of their dogs to her friend Karina's place in Salem while Jasper and Kinsley were honeymooning.

Karina owned a hobby farm with five acres. No doubt Gabe was having the time of his life. Dash, Jasper's K-9 partner, was staying with another officer in Tunnel Creek.

Noah finished the circle around the cabin, then motioned them over to the garage, where he used the pad beside the door to punch in a code. They cut through the garage, passing Kinsley's white SUV, then entered the laundry room. Once he shut the garage door, Noah led them into the kitchen.

Lucy gasped. The small tree his mom set up in the middle of the kitchen table caught her eye. "That's beautiful. It's so... joyful in here."

"My mom goes a little overboard at Christmas."

"I love it. Besides, there's no such thing as overboard at Christmas." Lucy ran her fingertips along a red-and-green Christmas plaque stenciled with a Bible verse about the birth of Jesus. "Did she make this?"

"She did."

"I'd love to learn how to do this." She dropped her hand.

"I'm sure my mom would teach you. She teaches art classes for adults and kids." He glanced at Boone. "She does crafts with Gabe all the time."

They walked through the kitchen and down the hall. Lucy oohed and aahed over his mom's handmade snowman figurines and her wreath wall. She even noticed the Christmas rug with different kinds of birds at the front door.

"That's Kinsley's. Anything with animals is hers."

Their nine-foot Douglas fir filled the front left corner of the living room, partially blocking one window. Homemade ornaments, large and small bulbs, tiny nativities and a silver-and-blue garland covered most of the tree.

"The tree is so pretty and festive. You guys should offer tours."

He snickered. "Don't give my mom any ideas."

Lucy walked along the edge of the room to check out the decorations as Boone found and opened one of Gabe's truck books.

Lucy circled back around to Noah. Her voice was low. "Should we look in his bag now?"

"Why don't you start that while I check upstairs. I'll be right back." He jogged up the stairs, opening closets and making sure windows were locked, then returned to the first floor.

Lucy had Boone's bag open, the contents laid out on the coffee table. The little talking dog, Mr. Barkey, was the biggest thing in there. A few army and outer space figurines spilled out along with a set of underclothes. She withdrew a tiny stuffed animal—another dog—then sat it between the other figures.

"Not much here."

"That's it?" He reached for the bag, but his arm brushed the white talking dog. It fell sideways, smacking the wood floors with a *clunk*.

A garbled man's voice filled the room.

"What're you doing with that? What does she have?"

"I don't know." Another man's voice, this one much clearer. Noah's throat closed. Was that Shawn?

"Get it from her."

"No!" A woman's high-pitched voice this time. "You won't get away with this!"

"Mommy?" Boone's small body jerked to attention across the living room. "Is that Mommy?"

A *whooshing* sound followed on the recording device, then a loud *clunk*. Similar to the sound of the plastic animal falling to the floor just now. Had his mom thrown the toy?

Lucy hurried over to Boone, stroking his arms. "Hey, let's go get something to eat in the kitchen." She shot Noah a pained, wide-eyed look. He gave a single nod, then lifted the recording toy from the ground as Lucy hurried the child from the room.

Noah inspected the plastic dog. Every

event from the last two days crystallized. *This* was what they were after.

An innocent child's toy had been used to record the voices of the man—men—who murdered Ryan Harrington. And those men were clearly willing to kill to get rid of it.

"Ms. Lucy?"

Lucy startled awake in the large, wood-framed bed. "Hey, Boone." She blinked groggily at their surroundings. Faint light trickled through the single window in the room. A small alarm clock read 7:18 a.m. They were in Noah's room, while he had taken over Jasper's room down the hall.

"I'm hungry."

"Again?" she teased. They'd eaten turkey and cheese sandwiches and apple slices last night, then she'd gotten Boone cleaned up and changed into Noah's nephew Gabe's clothes. When Lucy laid Boone down and rubbed his back on Noah's bed, she'd fallen asleep in the cozy spot, too. She and Noah hadn't gotten a chance to talk about the toy and what it meant for Boone and the crime.

She pulled her clean hair into a messy bun and released a long sigh. After washing up last night, Noah had offered her a pair of his mom's sweatpants and an art festival T-shirt. The simple, comfortable garments felt luxurious after days of wearing her dirty, stiff work clothes. Dana Holt even wore the same size shoe.

They treaded down the hall quietly, in case Noah was still sleeping. The bedroom door was most of the way closed, and she fought the urge to peek inside.

As they ascended the stairs, what happened last night replayed like a movie in her mind. The toy Boone called Mr. Barkey contained a voice recording from the night of Ryan Harrington's murder. Smart move from Boone's mom. She shook her head at the landing. Unbelievable.

Breakfast smells wafted over, and Boone took off down the hall. "Mr. Noah!"

Lucy followed him. Soft overhead lights and the muted morning sun illuminated

Noah, hard at work in the kitchen. A beeping oven warned that its contents were done. The scent of bacon teased her nose, and the toaster snapped four pieces of bread out.

Noah stood in the middle of it all, wearing an apron with a gray squirrel on the front and I'm Nuts About Cooking displayed beneath. She let out a burst of laughter.

"It's yummy in here!" Boone gripped the edge of the table and hopped on his tippy-toes like a hungry bunny.

"It sure is yummy in here. Thanks to Chef Noah."

"What, did the aroma of burnt toast wake you up?" He grinned at her, then his smile froze when their eyes connected. A jolt of awareness passed between them, an invisible rope drawing her to him. What in the world? She quickly shifted her focus to Boone.

"Actually, it was the five-year-old human alarm clock." She tickled Boone's side, and he giggled and jumped away from the table. She chanced a quick look at Noah again. He was—or had been—a stranger who put his life on the line for them. His kindness and caring manner made the terrible situation that much more bearable. The fact that he was handsome, too, was irrelevant.

Wasn't it?

Yes. She shook the unexpected thoughts away. Noah Holt would never go for a city girl like her, and she could *not* see herself with a man who would rather be outside than in. Especially now that she had a chance at the supervisory position in Greenville.

"I'm hungry." Boone grabbed the half-full bread basket.

Noah handed him a piece of buttered toast. "Eat that to tide you over."

He motioned them to the rectangular white table, where Boone wolfed the bread down. Noah set a glass of juice beside him, and it was gone in seconds, too.

"I have to go to the bathroom." The

child bounded off his seat and did his potty dance.

"Down this hall." Noah ushered him through the doorway and down the hallway. Lucy wandered over to the stove to see what was cooking. Eggs. A whole lot, she noted. Noah returned to the kitchen and leaned against the counter as he tended to the mountain of scrambled eggs in the skillet.

Lucy stared pointedly at the full frying pan. "Looks like you raided a hen house."

"Pretty much. I made extra in case you all are as hungry as I am."

"I'm definitely hungry. Thank you. Can I help with anything?"

"Here, you turn the eggs. I'll start more toast." He handed her the spatula. She took the utensil and moved past him, ignoring the warmth from his fingers as he handed it off.

Noah opened the large stainless-steel fridge and retrieved two more pieces of bread, then pushed them down in the toaster. He turned toward her, and a question popped into her mind.

"Is there a landline here?"

"No landline, sorry." His face fell.

"I really need to call Melissa."

"Melissa is your supervisor?"

"Yes. Here, they're done." She scooped the scrambled eggs into a large white bowl then set the spatula in the sink. "I'm sure she's worried sick. She was going to take Boone but ended up having out-of-town family stay over."

"Jasper said his work cell was here, but I can't find it. Until then, I'm sorry, you'll have to wait to call her." His mouth twisted. "I listened to the recording again last night, and I'm pretty sure one of those voices is Shawn Baxter."

"I'm sorry. Then he did betray you."

"Appears that way." Noah's brow creased. "I even wonder if he had something to do with the expired EpiPen."

Her mouth opened then closed. "That's terrible if he did that on purpose. Any ideas about the other voice?"

"Hard to tell. It's so garbled. I listened two more times and couldn't make it out. Still, that toy is most definitely evidence. It's exactly what they wanted from Boone."

"Yes."

Boone trotted back down the hall, and they settled in at the table. Noah said grace. The food was gone in less than five minutes, then the boy asked to go play in the front room. Lucy told him that was fine, then started picking up dishes. Boone was thrilled to play with Gabe's books and LEGO toys stashed in a basket between the couches.

"I'll do the dishes," she offered. "You cooked."

"If you insist." He gave a lighthearted shrug, and she tried not to stare. This Noah was so different from the serious, focused man who pulled them from her car on the river. Not better or worse, just different.

Noah helped carry the dishes to the sink as Lucy ran hot water and squirted soap onto a dishcloth. As bubbles covered her hands, another question came to mind.

"Your dad... What happened?"

Noah didn't answer for several moments. Had she overstepped? Finally, he turned so his lower back pressed into the counter. He crossed his arms. "My parents were missionaries in Cameroon. Dad was out visiting a family at another village. Bringing medical supplies and clothes. It was quite a distance from our mission guesthouse. He got lost on the way back, ended up in the jungle."

Her full stomach turned, and she stopped washing. "How sad. Did he...?"

"Die out there? Yes. We found him a couple weeks later. It was awful for my mom. She'd almost gone along but he talked her out of it. Mom lived with the what-ifs for a long time."

"Oh, Noah. That's terrible. Your poor mom. And you." Lucy dried her hands on the dish towel, then set a palm on his forearm. He stared down at where their skin connected for long moments before meeting her eyes, his face a mask of grief.

"I'm so sorry." She gazed across the kitchen, at the verse about Jesus's birth. "I've struggled with my faith ever since my parents' divorce." She angled her face toward him. "But your situation... How do *you* still have faith in God?"

"I guess the thought of *not* believing feels impossible." His mouth tilted in an ironic smile. "After Dad died, I was angry. Lost. Mad at the world, and missing him. We moved back to the States, and my mom urged me to find out what Dad loved. Said that would honor his life best, not the anger. I thought it was stupid at first."

She waited as he worked through the difficult memories.

"Eventually I opened his Bible, learned his favorite verses, found out what he loved most." He glanced at the ceiling, and the strong column of his throat bobbed in a swallow. "My dad loved God's creation, loved being outside. And now I do, too."

"I'm certain he would be incredibly proud of you." Lucy slowly drew her hand away.

"'From the end of the earth will I cry unto thee, when my heart is overwhelmed: lead me to the rock that is higher than I. For thou hast been a shelter for me, and a strong tower from the enemy.'"

She tilted her head. "You memorized that."

"It was one of my dad's life verses."

She shivered as a chill washed over her. "I've never thought of God as a shelter before."

"He is. He shelters us with His love. God does care about you, Lucy." He peered down the hall. "Both of you." His lips compressed into a frown. "Seems kind of cold in here. Where did Boone go?"

"The front room to read Gabe's books."

He pushed off the counter and strode down the hall. Lucy hurried after him.

The front room was wide and sunlight poured in through two windows on either side, highlighting the massive Christmas tree. In between the windows, the front door was flung open. Noah surged forward. Lucy followed, her heart sinking like an anchor in deep water. Through the window, she noticed a black truck parked a ways down the driveway.

"Someone is out there." Noah whipped around and started for the stairs. "Stay inside, I'm getting Jasper's gun."

He rushed up the stairs, taking them two at a time. Lucy pressed her palm to her chest as a man exited the black truck and ran at Boone, who appeared to be chasing after the birds at the bird feeder beside Noah's mom's art studio.

"Boone!"

She couldn't let the men get to him. Lucy burst through the front door, sprinting toward Boone. Cold air filled her lungs. The boy looked up at her with surprised, saucer-plate eyes.

"Ms. Lucy? I saw a squirrel and I—"

"Boone. Get inside!" She picked him up then pivoted to run back into the cabin.

The wind was knocked out of her as

strong arms grabbed her midstride. A scream ripped from her throat. "Noah, help! Get away from me!" She released Boone then tried to kick and punch her attacker, but the man subdued her arms and dragged her down the driveway, closer to the truck. She kicked at the ground and yelled at Boone.

"Boone! Run!"

"Get the kid now! Lady, I'm getting sick of going after you."

"Let me go!"

"Not this time."

The blond man scurried over to snatch Boone. *No!* From the corner of her eye, movement caught her attention near the front of the house. *Noah?*

Her kidnapper reached the truck, heaving her into the back seat. Boone landed on top of her, his pointy elbow jabbing her throat. Lucy choked on her scream as they slammed the back door then jumped in the front.

"Go, go, go!" one of them yelled.

The truck skidded down the hilly, snowy

driveway at a frightening speed. She and Boone rolled onto the floor beneath the back seat, squishing together.

Boone sniffled against her, and she managed to wrap an arm around him. What if she opened the door and they jumped? But where? Plus, exiting a moving vehicle was too dangerous now, especially for the small child.

Could Noah use his sister-in-law's car to come after them? Her stomach clenched so hard nausea climbed her throat. *Would it be in time?*

ELEVEN

Noah slammed into Kinsley's small SUV, parked in the cabin's garage. Jasper had left his Jeep at the airport before their honeymoon, and their mom drove her SUV to Karina's with Gabe and the dogs inside.

He ground his hands around the steering wheel as he backed out. He should've gone outside first, instead of getting his weapon. But he hadn't seen the second man, and hadn't considered the fact that if they got Lucy and Boone, he couldn't shoot and risk injuring either of them.

Something Lucy mentioned yesterday blazed through his thoughts as quickly as the vehicle speeding down the driveway. *The mine.* Could the men be taking them to Shadow Back Mine? But why? It was closed, even the small historical village nearby was shut down for renovations.

"God, please help me find them."

Fifteen minutes later, he pulled into the mine's visitor lot. Shadow Back Mountain's craggy, eaten-away peak rose into the sky like a giant anthill. Sure enough, the black truck was parked on the far side of the parking lot. Near the valley side. Thank the Lord his gut had been correct and the men hadn't considered that Lucy overheard and told him about the location they'd discussed.

He looked for a hidden spot to leave the SUV. *There.* A space behind a large red-and-brown outbuilding that served as the ticket booth for the mine and historical valley. Trees bookended the structure, offering more cover. Kinsley's small SUV would blend in nicely. He backed in carefully, then put it in Park. Noah gripped Jasper's spare Glock as he exited the vehicle and snuck around the back of the ticket booth.

Where were they? On the right sat

Shadow Back Mountain; the copper mine entrance was tightly barred to keep visitors out. Not likely there. To his left, in the far distance, the outline of black metal fences and small antiquated buildings broke the horizon. The tiny mining town of Shadow Back. Lots of places to hide kidnapped victims.

Noah clipped his teeth together as a bitter wind whipped across the valley.

He set out across the parking lot, heading toward the little village with its post office, a dozen small cabin-like houses, a white spired church and a red clapboard school. Local schools brought students here on field trips and families visited during the fall, when the hills surrounding the valley blazed with red, gold and orange foliage.

But the beauty of this area couldn't calm his raging pulse. He had to find them.

Noah kept to small clusters of trees until he reached the edge of the valley. There he found the remnants of the old road that used to connect the mine with the town. Nowadays, visitor buses took tourists back and forth, but tracks were overgrown since the mine's closure.

He crouched, inspecting the faint outline of any visible tire tracks. Despite the light dusting of snow, the earth didn't lie. Fresh truck treads showed the recent arrival of a vehicle. *The men must've driven Lucy and Boone over to the village then parked.*

Please, God, help me find them.

He stood and sprinted along the tire tracks, his chest rising and falling with each stride. His legs burned. He passed an old homestead, then another. Portions of fences still stood, bisecting the homesteads. An old barn sat far off to his left. Some of the houses had no glass in their windows, giving them an impression of open, lifeless eyes.

A prickle of alarm shot down his limbs. *Stop it, Holt. Focus.*

He neared the center of the old town, then darted behind an outhouse as men's voices carried over. Where were they coming from? The post office and old general store sat nearby, across the street from a crumbling black fence surrounding a small field of crooked tombstones.

Two men strode out of the post office, bickering back and forth. The door slammed as they took the porch steps and entered the road.

"We do what he asks us then we get the rest of the money. Simple as that."

"I didn't sign up to chase some kid through the woods." The shorter man gestured angrily. "I'm done after this. Done."

"Fine. Then you're done. Good riddance."

Noah held his breath as they crossed in front of the outhouse, only twenty or so yards away. He shimmied around the tall, narrow structure so they wouldn't see him.

"This was supposed to be a one-day job. We're working on a week here, man. We should just get rid of them."

"No. We do what the Big Man says. Then we get paid."

Noah peered at the buildings. Where were Lucy and Boone, in the post office? At one time, the post office had a back room used as a jail cell when someone was arrested in Shadow Back. Was it possible Lucy and Boone were in there?

The men took off the way Noah had just come. Sweat gathered on his brows, trickling down his neck. He'd made it just in time. *Thank You, Lord.* He said another prayer that they wouldn't see Kinsley's SUV behind the building.

He glanced at the graveyard. A massive cherrybark oak tree leaned over the tombstones like a giant, its branch arms spread out midair like it was trying to reach for the worn blocks that marked where miners and their families had lived and died.

Goose bumps prickled his scalp. He'd always liked visiting Shadow Back Mine and this little town, but right now an eerie and constant sense of danger kept his nerves on fire.

Noah waited until the men climbed into the vehicle in the distance and the truck disappeared from the parking lot. Then he shot across the road, straight into the post office. Chairs and tables littered the space. What a mess. Food containers. Soda cans. Trash. Had someone been living here?

A sniffle caught his attention through a set of swinging double doors. Lucy?

He checked through the window, then hurried to the back of the building. Pushing through the doors, he met Lucy's eyes from behind the bars of the former jail cell.

"Noah!"

"Mr. Noah! See, God brought him to find us."

He rushed to the bars, and Boone stuck his thin arms through first. Noah squeezed them.

"Hey, buddy. God brought me here, alright."

Lucy reached for his hands. He gripped one of Boone's, then Lucy's. Her slim fingers threaded with his, and his heart double-timed.

"You found us."

"I'm sorry they got you. I couldn't risk—"

"It's okay, Noah. I know. You didn't want to shoot because we were in the back seat. I get it."

His gaze bounced throughout the room.

"They took the keys," she explained. "I saw the shorter one pocket them before they walked out."

He nodded, figuring as much. A quick inspection confirmed there was no other way inside the jail cell. The square window on the wall caught his eye. The triple bars that had once crowded the frame had long since rusted away, leaving only glass behind. He released their hands, met her eyes.

"Both of you need to get as far away from the window as you can."

"Noah! Where are you…?"

Her question faded as he exited the building at a jog, then raced around back. On the side of the structure, a large branch lay beneath a pair of oaks set beside the post office. That would work. He found the high window and tapped the branch on the thin pane of glass to warn her. Once more.

"Watch out!" he shouted, then swung. The first hit cracked the glass, but it held in place. He swung it a second time, and it shattered inside the jail cell.

Moments later Boone's face appeared. Lucy must be lifting him up and out.

"I'm here. Send him through."

Noah spread his arms out and planted his feet as the child climbed into the open window. Boone stared down from the eight-foot height, his little face scrunched up in fear.

"Mr. Noah, it's too high."

"It's okay, I'll catch you." He grinned up at him. "You're tough, Boone. You can do this."

A moment later, Boone launched from the small ledge, dropped directly at Noah. He grabbed the child to his chest, wrapping his arms tight. They both gasped at the impact.

"You did it. You were flying like a bird."

He chucked his chin. "Just don't do that again."

He set Boone down, then looked up to see Lucy's face appear. She struggled into the opening, her eyes fearful and her mouth open with the effort of climbing.

"Noah, are you sure...?"

"I've got you. I won't let you hit the ground."

The next thing he knew, Lucy maneuvered so her legs pushed through, then her torso. She turned, her stomach against the building, then called down.

"Here I come." She dropped immediately, and he clasped her falling form to himself, her back to his chest. He padded her landing so her feet barely brushed the ground. Once her momentum stopped, she turned in his protective embrace.

He kept his arms around her, and she did the same. "Thank you for coming for us."

"I wasn't going to leave you."

She sagged into him, and he realized he was holding her upright.

"Hey, you did it. Remember, brave

Lucy? That's you. You didn't even look twice." He settled her on her feet.

"I knew you'd catch me." She pushed carefully away from him.

"I hope your faith in me isn't misplaced."

"It isn't." She gave him a brief, wide smile, and his chest hitched.

Lucy had proven her courage throughout their ordeal, along with her caring heart for Boone, but she was about as far from an ideal match as could be. Her dislike of the woods was an impassable mountain between them. After Tessa's rejection, he wasn't taking a chance again with someone so vastly different. Plus, hadn't Lucy said she was hoping to get a promotion and move back to Greenville?

Noah shook that train of thought away and stepped back. "We need to get you two out of here. I'm in the parking lot at the mine."

They jogged away from the post office. The remaining snow crunched underfoot. Noah set his palm on Boone's shoulder to guide him as the child meandered to the right instead of straight toward the faded roadway leading back to the parking lot.

"You got to be in a real jail cell, Boone. Like an outlaw from the Wild West."

He puffed up his small chest. "Look at me. I'm an outlaw." Boone pointed at the graveyard. "What is that?"

Noah and Lucy shared a quick, loaded look.

"Look at the big tree. Can I play on it?" Boone stuck out his arm, distracted before they had to answer about the graveyard. The child beelined for the immense claw-like roots surrounding the gigantic tree.

"Boone, stay close," Noah warned, following the child into the sea of oak roots, dirt and leftover snow. "Come away from there."

Boone yelped, and in that second, time slowed. Lucy called out from behind him, some sort of warning, just as Noah realized Boone wasn't standing to his full height. No, his feet appeared partially stuck below the roots. Noah looked down as the dirt shifted below his own feet. What was happening?

Boone screeched when his small body dropped even lower. "The mud is getting me!"

"Noah, what is happening?" Lucy cried.

Noah's heart roared in his chest. A sinkhole? Recent heavy storms plus the cooled earth must've expanded the soil enough that it lifted the roots. Made the ground unstable.

Noah leapfrogged toward Boone. Was his weight too much? The huge root ball, easily the size of a box truck, shuddered below him. More dark, wet dirt fell belowground, opening up spaces where Boone or he could fall through.

Lucy paced the far edge of the sinkhole as Noah neared the child. His muscles trembled under the strain.

"Boone. Jump toward me, just like the window."

A shuddering, ghastly creaking sound released from below them. Noah leaped at Boone, tucking the child into a tight embrace then landing in a crouch so he could gain power and launch away. His leap fell short as the massive tree rose and groaned out a hundred years of life coming to an end. The motion lifted Noah, slamming him backward into the trunk.

They careened sideways as the root system loosened. The ground gaped wide, forcing him and the child lower. Noah shouted. Cold, wet dirt covered his arms and legs as they fell down, down into darkness. Swallowed into the bowels of the earth.

Please, God...

Lucy's scream was drowned out by the soil piling around him and Boone.

Lucy couldn't breathe. Couldn't think. Couldn't believe they were gone. She inched as close as she could to the gaping hole, but the ground felt shaky. Unstable. The base of the tree, all the roots, stuck in the air like a giant gnarled hand. A hand that had taken Noah and Boone.

Tears obscured the mangled root system. Everything looked dark down below.

The huge tree had fallen across the graveyard, crashing into the black metal gate and crushing a few tombstones.

"Please, God, let them be alive." She backed onto the road. Where could she get help? Not the men who kidnapped them. Lucy swiped away the tears and gazed around. The valley was eerily silent, the only sounds occasional bursts of wind and the lonely caw of a crow in the distance. She'd never felt so alone. But Boone was with the most capable man she'd ever met. Noah would find a way out. But where? Were there air pockets they could breathe in?

"God, help me!" A sob wrenched from the depths of her soul. "How do I get them out?"

A squirrel chirped angrily nearby. She turned, her heart double-thumping. It must've been on the big tree when it fell. The small gray animal scurried along a thick, gnarled tree branch that thrust out over the road. It scrambled down the length of the branch, jumped to the ground, then darted past her, running toward the post office. Then the squirrel climbed a tree beside that building.

Was there a phone inside? She'd been so upset at their capture and being shoved in the cell she hadn't looked. Lucy sprinted to the post office then flew up the steps.

The floor creaked beneath her weight as she entered. A dusty card table with brochures sat beside the entrance, a pair of empty chairs just past that. Old black-and-white pictures covered the walls, and a large double window sat on the wall opposite the door. To her left was the doorway leading to the back of the post office, where she and Boone had been held in the cell. She traced the perimeter of the room, keeping an eye out for any type of phone.

Please, God. It had been at least two minutes since they'd disappeared beneath the ground.

Another door caught her eye and she hurried across the room, her body shaking like a leaf in the wind. Was this a closet? She turned the knob, but the door wouldn't budge. She dug her heels in and pulled harder. The hinges creaked, bowing slightly until the door flew open. Lucy was thrown back, and her heels slipped on the ratty rug lying in the center of the room.

She fell, her backside landing hard on the edge of the frayed rug. A compact, hard edge beneath its material dug into her skin.

She flung the dirty gray-and-blue rug away. Was there a basement beneath this building? Hope flared hot, stinging her eyes. Had Boone and Noah fallen down there? Could she get to them this way?

A metal handle stuck up about a quarter of an inch from the flat floor. That must be what had indented her skin. She slipped a finger underneath it then lifted. It groaned in protest, then shifted slightly. Inserting three fingers and positioning herself with leverage to use her legs, she tugged again. Her shoulders strained, and an ache spread down her back. The door must weigh forty or fifty pounds, or else hadn't been opened in years.

A muffled shout carried up from the floor. She let go, flailing back, her heart lodged in her throat. Who was that? It sounded like the person said her name. Could it be Noah? She rose to her knees and continued tugging until her muscles burned and tears drenched her cheeks.

God, give me strength.

Darkness and dirt blotted out Noah's senses. He rose on unsteady legs, cradling Boone to his chest. All he could smell and taste was the earth. Mud. Cold, stale air surrounded them. His nightmare scenario played out in frightening real time. Claustrophobia.

He hated being stuck inside tight spaces. Now wasn't a time to panic. Boone needed him to be strong. Needed Noah to get them out of here. He coughed and gagged, spitting grimy bits of stone and grit off his tongue.

They'd landed on a pile of loosened dirt, which had cushioned the drop. Whatever chasm they'd fallen into, it had enough room that they could move and breathe. Thank the Lord for that.

"I can't see," Boone said.

"I'm here, buddy. I got you." Noah drew in slow breaths of cold, stale air through his nose to combat the terrorizing feeling of being stuck in a cramped, dark place. He flicked a small stone out of his ear.

"It smells bad."

"It sure does. We'll need a bath after this. A long one, with extra soap." A faint shaft of daylight stole down through the opening above, but otherwise the space was pitch-dark. "Do you have dirt in your eyes or mouth? Spit it out. And pick it out of your nose."

"You want me to pick my nose?"

"Yes." His smile felt more like a grimace. "Get the dirt out."

He helped wipe the remaining dirt from the boy's face, relieved to see the steady rise and fall of Boone's chest. No wheezing. He pushed through the panic clutching his rib cage to focus on Boone and their situation. He had to figure out where they were. They'd sunk into some sort of manhole. Or cave, or was it…a tunnel?

Lucy. Did she think they were dead, that they'd been buried alive? He hated the thought of her twenty feet up. Crying. Upset. Was she digging around the root system, looking for them?

Digging. The copper mine. Noah's eyes widened. Could this be an old mining shaft?

"I'm c-cold." Boone shivered.

Noah tightened his hold on the child. "I'll keep you warm. Snuggle up." He infused his voice with as much enthusiasm as he could muster. "Guess what you did? You discovered a mining tunnel."

"Mining?" Boone repeated.

"It's where men dig underground for gold and precious metals like what ladies' rings are made from. This is an old mine shaft. They looked for copper here."

"I don't want copper." Boone set his

cheek to Noah's neck as he inched along the corridor. "I want Ms. Lucy."

"Me, too." He wanted to find her, and let her know they were okay. He wanted to keep her safe, too. That was it. The fact that she was as lovely as a mountain sunrise didn't matter.

Especially since she hated said mountains and their sunrises. Hated the woods. Not that he could blame her. It sounded like the camping situation with her parents had traumatized her. Cemented a lifetime dislike for the outdoors. It was too bad. But once Lucy and Boone were safely turned over to Jasper and the authorities, Noah's job was done.

He adjusted his grip on Boone as they inched forward. Unfortunately, the farther they traveled from the hole they'd fallen through, the darker it became. He didn't have a flashlight. Closing his eyes, Noah held still. His sense of direction had been a God-given gift, his mom had always said. Even Jasper had admitted Noah always knew which was north, south, east or west.

He kept his eyes shut and turned in a circle, then pointed. That was north. The other arm came out at the opposite direction. South. Right by the post office. An idea popped into his mind. Could the post office have an entry point to this tunnel? There had to be some way down here, otherwise why did the early settlers dig this tunnel out this far from the actual mine?

He'd had no idea the tunnels reached halfway across the valley.

Noah turned, heading southeast. Back toward the huge mound of earth they'd fallen into. He eyeballed it. If there were roots or something to climb, that might've worked. Instead, dirt piled most of the way to the ceiling. They were at least twenty feet belowground. Maybe more. He couldn't risk sinking back into the dirt.

No, it was best to see if there was another way out. He turned and headed toward what felt like the post office.

Which meant they were crossing below the old road.

Several steps later, the tunnel narrowed, and he had to duck to continue forward. Panic sucker punched him. *God, please help. Keep me breathing.*

He might not have asthma like Boone, but the sensation of being stuck in this closed-in, smelly, dark tunnel made it tough to draw a full breath.

The light thinned out so he could barely see an inch in front of his face. With each step, the roof lowered. He prayed the opening they'd fallen through now allowed more oxygen into this tight space.

The floor rose like they were walking on an incline, and soon he was fully crouching. His back ached at the position and holding the extra forty or fifty pounds of Boone. It had to be only five and a half feet tall. Noah shuddered, setting Boone on his feet, sucking in slow breaths through his nostrils.

Suddenly his hand struck something solid. A box? No, two or three of them.

Stacked tight. The tunnel shrank even more as he felt along the wall. Eight at final count. Were these old containers for mining? The metal felt...new. Not rusted. Clean.

Wait—was someone using this hidden space to store things?

He felt around one of the box tops, found a lid, lifted it and slipped his hand inside. Dozens of small, smooth, narrow objects clacked together into his palm.

Ice coursed through his veins. Bullets. Ammunition. These were ammo cans. The gun cartel, whose hiding spot Jasper discovered in Whisper Mountain Tunnel, was still running. And they'd found another hiding spot out here at Shadow Back Mountain. In the mines.

Shawn must be part of this.

"Where's Ms. Lucy? I want her."

"She's up there, looking for us." He was certain of that. She might not like the outdoors—his world—but she was smart and strong. Capable and caring. She wouldn't give up. "Let's pray she finds us."

"Okay."

Noah bowed his head beside Boone and said a quick prayer that Lucy would find an opening to the tunnel. Boone shouted *Amen* after he finished, and Noah chucked the child's chin softly.

"You are one strong kid, Boone. And the best way to be strong in this world is by trusting God." He looked up. "Let's keep moving forward. Might be a door up here."

Several steps later, a shadow rose out of the darkness. He slowed, his muscles tense. What was that? Then his boot knocked into a raised metal surface. Stairs. *Thank You, God.* His back ached from their awkward stooping position. When they climbed the first stair, he kept his palms out. Six steps later, he hit smack into what felt like a door.

Noah set Boone down on the stair below the one he crouched on. "Stay right there."

He ran his hands down the door, searching for hooks, knobs. Nails, bolts. Anything.

The smoothness of the solid surface dried out his mouth. Nothing. No knob. He pushed hard. The door didn't budge. Was this an entry point then, not an exit? Did that mean they were stuck here, between the pile of dirt and this old, immovable door?

What if they called out Lucy's name? Was it possible she'd hear them? He had to try.

"I'm going to yell for Ms. Lucy. Cover your ears."

Boone did as Noah told him, then Noah shouted her name. Over and over, for several seconds. Boone joined in, his little voice almost screaming. The hope that had resurrected when they'd hit the floor of the tunnel and fallen out of the dirt crumbled like the sinkhole had.

"Did she hear us?" Boone asked.

"I don't know." He dragged a hand through his dirty hair.

He waited for a few seconds, listening. But there was no answer above. Only silence. *Please, God, help us.*

TWELVE

Lucy. Had someone said her name? The volume was so faint, like the person was a dozen miles away, but it sounded like her name. Could it be... Noah? Boone?

She pulled harder, until her arms shook and a creak split the air. There. Dust exploded into the air as the door in the floor released a groan, its strong suction finally letting loose. Lucy fell backward, the momentum throwing her into the nearest wall. Pain throbbed along her spine as she hit the hard surface.

Noah burst up and out of the opening with a shout, Boone in his arms.

She stumbled upright. "Noah! Boone!" *Thank You, God.* She hurled herself at them, wrapping her arms around Noah's broad, dirty shoulders, enclosing Boone between them.

"You're alive!" One of Noah's arms came around her, and with her cheek pressed to his chest, there was no mistaking the powerful sound of his pounding heart.

"You found the door." Noah spoke into her hair. "I knew you could do it."

"It was hidden under a rug." She pulled back to look at the boy. "Boone! Oh, buddy, you're covered in dirt. That must've been so scary." She gently wiped the grit off his face and clothes. Tears wet her cheeks, but she didn't care. The thought of losing them had devastated her. Not because Boone was part of her caseload, but because she cared about him. About both of them.

Noah set Boone down so she could finish cleaning him up, then he ran a hand down his dirt-streaked face. "Ahh. So nice to breathe real air."

"I'm just glad you had *any* air down there." She folded to her knees in front of Boone. "Is your breathing okay?"

The child nodded. "Mr. Noah and I prayed you would find the door and you did."

"God showed me where to look." She pulled him close. "I'm so glad to see you, buddy. I'm so happy you're safe. It was horrible, so horrible, when you disappeared. Boone, you're okay? You're sure nothing hurts?"

"I'm squished." He squirmed in her embrace.

"I'm sorry, I was so worried." She let go of him then combed back his brown curls. Tiny pebbles fell from his scalp, and, from the looks of it, Noah's, too.

"It smelled yucky down there."

"I'm sure it did." She stood, meeting Noah's eyes. "Are you okay?"

"I am now." He shook off more mud and filth from his shoes. "I don't ever want to do that again."

"I'm so thankful Boone had you. I knew he had a chance because you were there."

"God got us out of there. And you." Noah wiped his jeans, then frowned. He reached into his pocket, withdrawing something small and gray. "Huh. Looks like I brought a piece of the mine shaft with me."

"What is that?"

He held out his hand. In the center of his large palm sat a small gray heart-shaped rock.

"Look at that. It's pretty."

"Here, you keep it." He handed it to her.

"Thank you." The stone's smooth edges pressed into her fingers as she placed it in the pocket of his mom's sweatpants. Then she shivered from the cold and from relief. "Where *were* you? Did you say that's a mine shaft?"

"It sure is." Noah shoved his hand through his hair, shaking out more dirt. "I didn't know they ran this far from the mine."

A lock of Noah's hair stuck out at a funny angle, and she reached up to brush it down. Their gazes collided, until heat climbed her neck.

He gave a lopsided grin. "Are *you* okay?"

"Now that you two are standing here, I am."

"Good. Listen, we need to get out of here. No telling when those men will return." He stretched his shoulders and back.

"What are those?" She motioned at a pair of crates pushed into a corner of the room. "Is this some sort of drug house?"

"Not drugs. Munitions. Bullets. They must've set up shop here after this place was closed. No doubt this is connected to what Jasper found at the Whisper Mountain Tunnel last year." He glanced pointedly at Boone. "His father was about to expose the players, specifically Shawn Baxter." He sighed. "And whoever else was on that recording toy."

"What if police can't make out the other voice?"

"I imagine a crime lab could analyze it, break it down enough to decipher the other player."

"I hope they can."

"Me, too. Boone, let's go." Noah headed

to the doorway leading out of the post office. When he opened it, two men pushed through. One dove for Noah, knocking the butt of his rifle against Noah's middle. He fell backward, righted himself, then lunged at his attacker. A second man appeared, punching him.

"No!" Lucy screamed, pushing Boone behind her.

Noah collapsed to the floor, blood trickling from his nose. She screamed again as the short, burly man stepped over Noah and strode toward her.

"You scream one more time, he dies." The man pointed the gun at Noah moaning on the ground. "Move. And don't even think about trying to escape."

Lucy's legs wobbled as they forced her and Boone out of the old post office. Two armed men stood outside, masks on and guns aimed their way.

A black truck sat a couple hundred yards away, far on the other side of the cemetery. Beside it, a nondescript white van was parked parallel. The van she'd ridden in when they took her and Boone to the water treatment facility.

"Don't try anything, or you're gonna end up in there." The blond kidnapper gestured to the graveyard with an oily snicker. He pushed her along. "How'd your Mountain Man know you were here?"

She grabbed Boone's hand, holding it tightly while glaring at her captors.

What were they doing with Noah? She turned just as the two other armed men went into the post office. Lucy's insides quaked. *Please, God. Protect him.*

Seconds later, they dragged him outside and followed the path Lucy and Boone were on with the other two men, toward the truck.

Where were they taking them now?

Noah struggled to drag himself from the abyss. His eyes opened, and he blinked several times to clear the grogginess away. Even then, everything remained dark. His head felt like a freight train was rolling over it again and again.

Had he been drugged? Where was he?

He cataloged the surroundings. He lay on a smelly couch in a small room, his wrists and ankles tied. Blinds covered the windows, and he was alone.

Where were Lucy and Boone, and were they okay?

Recent memories flashed through the fog in his mind. Shadow Back Mountain. Lucy and Boone. The sinkhole. A mining shaft. Another hidden cache of ammunition, just like at the Whisper Mountain Tunnel.

Then multiple men busting into the post office.

He stretched his shoulders and moved his feet, testing the rope's strength. Sharp pain spiderwebbed across his skull. They must've clocked him hard. Again.

Men's voices carried over. Noah strained to sit up, then listened. He shut out everything else—the rancid scent of filthy furniture and musty air, and the *ping-ping* of dripping water outside the window. Two voices tangled, arguing. A third broke in, silencing the first two.

An invisible fist squeezed his ribs. Just as he thought.

A door slammed, and then footsteps approached. He tensed.

"You are a hard man to catch."

Shawn Baxter stepped into the room, an irritated look on his face. His jet-black hair was combed back, and the beard he'd worn since Noah met him a few months earlier was shaved.

"What're you doing, Shawn?" He drilled the other man with a hot gaze. "Why're you part of this?"

Shawn rubbed his forehead. "All you had to do was *not* find them. Just let the men take care of—"

Noah jumped to his feet and threw himself at Shawn. The element of surprise was on his side as he knocked into the smaller, younger man.

They fell to the floor, but Noah's ropes held fast. Shawn swore and scrambled out of reach, then kicked Noah's stomach. Pain burst through his midsection.

"What is wrong with you? I tried to keep you from getting involved in this. Even planted a used EpiPen to get you suspended for a bit."

"Snake," he snarled. "Didn't work so well, did it? You're trying to kill a child. No decent human being would do such a thing."

Shawn stood over him, rubbing his palms together. "You have no idea what I've dealt with in my life. If I'd been a decent human being, I'd be dead."

"Look, I'm sorry you had a rough life. Mine wasn't exactly cake, either. But you have to understand that Boone and Lucy don't know anything."

"Don't lie to me. I know the kid has that voice recorder. His mom tricked us."

He wasn't about to let Shawn know they found out about Boone's toy and the evidence it held. "What are you talking about? They're innocent. The kid wasn't in the room when you murdered his dad."

"I'm not the one who pulled the trigger on Mr. Harrington."

"Who else is working with you besides these men?"

"What, you want on the roster now, too?"

"Never." Noah clenched his jaw. "Are you the *Big Man*?"

Shawn chuckled, the sound harsh instead of humorous. "Wouldn't you like to know."

"My gut stopped me from trusting you when you answered the radio. Guess I was right. You ratted us out at the fire tower, didn't you? You're a criminal."

Shawn kicked him again, but this time Noah pulled back enough to avoid a direct hit. "How's your gut feel now?"

Noah glared up at him from the dirty carpet. Where were Lucy and Boone? His coworker broke eye contact and held up his hands. "Don't look at me like that, Holt. You have no idea what you stepped into. No idea."

He did, actually, after finding those bullets. But playing dumb was the smartest way to go. "Why don't you tell me, then?"

"You know too much already, Mountain Man." Shawn pulled out a gun. "Move. I'm untying your ankles. You do anything stupid, the girl and that kid won't make it out of this house."

He yanked Noah's arms back, pulling him upright. Noah's shoulder joints screamed at the rough movements.

Shawn untied the ankle ropes then pushed him toward the doorway. "Walk."

Noah's eyes roved around. Looking for anything identifiable. Narrow, dark halls. Old wood and carpet floors, marked by age and use. Small windows. It appeared to be an older one-story house, the walls decorated with faded pink flowery wallpaper reminiscent of the early '90s. They passed another room, and the sound of soft crying burned his ears.

"Lucy." His pulse skyrocketed when he saw her tied up and seated in an empty room. Shawn shoved him so he couldn't get a good look. "Where's Boone?"

"Noah," she cried. "He's with me."

Noah slowed, trying again to see into the room, but Shawn thrust him forward.

"Mr. Noah!" Boone's little voice invigorated Noah's senses. He shook his head and focused. There had to be a way to distract these men and get the two of them out of here.

"What is this, a lovers' reunion?" Shawn sneered. "You just met her."

The short, burly man appeared at the end of the hall, his ugly smile growing when he spotted Noah. "Didn't get away this time, did ya?"

Noah jutted his chin at the white bandage wrapped around the man's arm, where Noah's bullet had nicked him that night in the ranger cabin. "At least one of us has good aim."

"Shut up," the shorter man growled. "I'll be paying you back for that real soon."

He and Shawn entered a large open room, likely the living and dining room for the house. A couple desks were set up, spread a few feet apart. Food storage containers, soda cans, boxes and paperwork littered the tops.

"What are you doing with them?" Noah asked.

"Don't you worry. All three of you will be with the police very soon."

"What?" Noah jerked back. How could they do that, after all the men had done? A dark sense of foreboding slithered through his mind. "Who's handing us over to police?"

A thin blond man entered the house through the front door. His eyes widened seeing Noah standing there, then a cocky grin covered his face.

"We're going through with the plan." Shawn addressed the two men. "Call me when it's done."

"What plan?" Noah demanded.

The blond man coughed to cover a chuckle, then bent over when he couldn't stop laughing. "Like we're gonna tell you."

The burly criminal turned to Shawn. "You're sure we do this now?"

"Yes, you idiot. Get it done."

Noah gulped down a breath. "*Who* is handing us over to the police?"

The blond man smiled at him, the creepy gesture showing his mottled green teeth. "It won't be us, Mountain Man. See, the police are going to find all three of you inside that lady's car on the river. Drowned."

Lucy tried to listen as Noah was taken to the front of the house. Their voices were too muffled, the words incoherent. Tears welled in her eyes at the expression Noah had worn on his face. Desperation. Anger. Worry.

A door slammed, and Boone trembled beside her. "I want to go away from here."

"Me, too, buddy." She twisted her head, eyeing the items in the room. There was very little. Two chairs, a long table pushed up against the small rectangular window framed by dusty pink curtains. Had this room once been a bedroom that belonged to a child? And now killers and criminals used it for nefarious purposes.

Killers.

Her mind stumbled over the reality of their situation. These men wouldn't turn them in. They'd—

"Hey, pretty lady. Time to move."

She struggled against the stocky man's hold. "We don't know anything. Let us go!"

"Not happening. And your ranger hero isn't going to save you this time." He squeezed her upper arm so hard it pinched her muscle. She bit back a cry.

"Now, don't try getting away this time. We wouldn't want this little boy getting hurt, would we?"

He loosened his hold, but still gripped her too tightly. He wasn't letting go. Not this time.

"Please," she murmured. "He's five. He doesn't remember anything about that night—"

"Nick, shut her up and get them out here," someone called from the front room.

"Hear that? Clamp it, lady." The short man holding her hostage—Nick—wrapped his arm through hers and propelled her forward. If only she could get Boone loose, let him escape. But where were they? Where would they go?

When they approached the front door, Nick turned, his dark flat eyes filled with hatred. "If you scream, someone's going to get hurt."

He dragged her outside, down a front porch with broken railing and three creaky, rotted steps. She almost pitched forward keeping up with his relentless pace. Thick woods surrounded them, no other houses in sight. He opened the double back doors of the white van, then shoved her inside and pushed her down into a bucket seat at the back of the vehicle. The blond man guarded the back when the shorter man retraced his steps into the abandoned house.

She studied the inside of the vehicle. Not much inside. Dark tint on the windows would keep them hidden if they passed other cars.

Nick returned moments later with Boone, sitting the boy down beside her.

"I'm here, buddy," she whispered. "How's your breathing?"

"Okay. Where are we going?"

Her chest felt like it was caving in. Most likely they were headed to their deaths.

"I'm not sure, but I want you to know I love you and I'm not going to leave you. I'm here with you." As the words left her lips, she realized they were the very words she'd longed to hear from her own mom and dad as a child. When they'd separated and their family had cracked apart. She'd needed to know she wasn't alone in the midst of the chaos of her life.

But she hadn't been alone. God was always with her. He loved her. Valued her. Made her, in fact. She was certain of that now, without a doubt. He'd shown Himself faithful so far, and He would again. And He loved and valued Boone.

The boy deserved to feel safe, even during this horrible time.

Lucy's teeth clenched when the vehicle rolled over a bumpy spot in the driveway.

Where were they taking them? *Please, God, keep Boone and me safe. And Noah.* Where was Noah?

Her thoughts turned to the stoic, honorable ranger she'd had trouble trusting the first few hours after he'd found them in the river. How he'd saved them, then protected them time and time again. Her throat closed as she considered all he'd done for them. The terrible situation he'd been dragged into while helping them.

"I'm c-cold," Boone whispered.

"I know, I am, too." She moved closer to him, her gaze on the driver, Nick. Every now and then he'd dart warning looks back at them, his face a mask of impatient anger. She understood enough about crime to know the fact they'd seen their faces didn't bode well for their outcome.

No. She wouldn't let herself go there.

They would get away. Somehow. Some way. They had to. She craned her neck, trying to see the row in front of her, then gasped softly.

Noah lay on the seat two rows up, his

large frame curled on his side on the bench seat.

Was he awake, or had they knocked him out again? She half rose to get a better look. They must've brought him in the van before her. Having him close by fortified her determination and gave her hope. He'd called her brave in the forest, and she would be now. Had to.

How could she distract Nick, the driver? She peered at him. He wasn't paying attention. Still, Lucy didn't want to chance bringing trouble on the child. Boone had been through so much the last few days. The loss of his dad. His mom in the hospital. All this danger the last few days in the woods.

If she'd gone through what he had, she would be in a corner, crying until she...

Crying. What if Boone pretended to cry, like he had to go to the bathroom? Could this work?

She leaned sideways, her cheek resting on Boone's head. A wave of affection for this resilient child crashed over her. Would he understand?

"Boone, can you pretend to cry?" She angled her face so they made eye contact. The boy's big brown eyes widened. "Can you do that for me?"

"I did before."

"Do it again. Louder." She glanced ahead. The men had country music playing, and they bickered back and forth. "Pretend you have to go potty. Or your stomach is upset. We don't want to be with these men."

"They're bad."

"Yes, very bad."

Boone sent a frown at the men, then he snuffled through his nose a couple times. A soft cry followed. While she knew him well enough to recognize it was fake, the men didn't. Sure enough, the noise caught the driver's attention.

"What is wrong with that kid now?" the blonde man grumbled.

Nick laughed. "He's just being a crybaby."

They drove for another minute or so, then Lucy nudged Boone. "Keep trying. Please."

The boy nodded, his lip curling under as though they'd legitimately hurt his feelings. He let out a long, ear-piercing wail then sniffled a few times for good measure.

"Hey, kid. Shut it," Nick warned, making a round-eyed, angry face in the mirror at Boone.

The blond man gestured. "You were supposed to turn left back there."

"No, I wasn't," Nick shot back. "Shut up. I know where I'm going."

Whatever frustration had been building between the two men poured out in their heated conversation. Lucy flinched. If only she could cover Boone's ears. They argued for several seconds, until Boone whimpered again.

"I have to go potty," he whined loudly.

"What in the—" the driver snarled as he pulled the van onto the shoulder. The wheels bumped over uneven ground, sending Lucy crashing into Boone. They both cried out as they nearly slid off the seat. A resounding thud came from directly in front of her.

Had Noah fallen to the van floor?

"Hey, watch out!" the blond man shouted.

Nick hit the brakes, and the van slid toward a large tree. The front bumper bumped into it, and Nick let out a string of colorful words.

"What're you doing? We're gonna get stuck here!" the blond man yelled.

"What'd you want me to do, let the kid make a mess in my van?"

"It's just a van, Nick. Now you hit a tree."

"You know what, I wanna finish the job here, Donny. I'm sick of dealing with them. And I'm sick of dealing with you."

Her skin prickled with goose bumps. *No.*

"No way." The other man, Donny, shook his head. "It's not part of the plan. I want the rest of the money. We do it right."

Nick and Donny. She committed their

names to memory as the men exited the vehicle, their doors slamming simultaneously. Lucy jolted in the seat when something touched her ankle. Noah? His fingers wrapped around her ankle, a gentle pressure. Reassurance. Had his hands come free?

He released her as the men's voices rose in volume. Then the side door opened, jarring her senses. Cold air flooded the interior. The blond man—Donny—appeared, leering at her.

"What're you doing on the floor?" Nick questioned Noah. "Donny, why's he on the floor?"

"Because of your bad driving," Donny shot back.

Nick glared at Donny, then addressed them. "Don't get any ideas, you two." The man eyed Lucy and Noah, then snatched Boone across her lap, dragging the boy out of the vehicle. "I'm gonna untie your hands, kid. Do your business over there. You run off, a bear will get you. Got it? Hurry up."

Lucy tried to see what was going on, but the men had shut the door.

"My hands are loose." Noah's fingers returned to her ankle, exerting gentle pressure. "Problem is I can't get you and Boone out at the same time. Not sure I can take those men on."

"Take Boone. Get him and get out of here." The words cost a great deal, but she was certain it was the best route for their situation. "They don't want me, they want him."

"Lucy."

"Get Boone to your brother. They don't want me, so..."

"They're taking us back to your car, on the Broken Branch River. It must not have sunk yet. It was jammed on a rock when I saw it last. They're going to kill us then make it look like we drowned." He paused. "They don't know I called Jasper."

She scored her palms with her nails. "You have to find a way out of here. Please, Noah. Take Boone."

"I'm not leaving you, Lucy."

The words she'd longed to hear as a child settled into the lonely crevices of her heart, as solid and real as the small heart-shaped stone Noah gave her that was still nestled in her pocket.

Tears threatened, and she blinked them away. "Okay. So, what do we do?"

A shout echoed off the van windows, stopping Noah's next words.

"Get him!" one of the men yelled.

"Boone took off," Noah said in wonder.

He struggled on the grungy van floor, grunting as he wrestled with something. "There's a seat stabilizer down here. I'll use it to cut these. Once I get the rope off my ankles, I'll grab the tire iron back here on the floor."

He struggled for several seconds as she craned her neck to see what was happening outside. *Please, God, protect Boone.* Her lungs constricted. What if they caught him and decided to… She clenched her eyes shut. No, she wouldn't let her mind go there.

"Got it." Noah's head and shoulders

popped up. With deft movements, he worked at the rope on her wrists. Lucy leaned into him, assured he wouldn't hurt her. He was so different from any other man she'd known. She never doubted his care. Never questioned his intentions.

"Done."

"Thank you." She shook away the ropes and freed her wrists.

Noah peered through the van windows. "When we jump out of this vehicle, I have no idea who or what is out there. Or where we are exactly."

She nodded, her mouth as dry as cotton. This was their only chance.

"We'll have to run again. Let me worry about Boone. You pick a direction and take off. Hide somewhere safe. I'll find you."

"I know."

He glanced her way, and their gazes fused tight. "Brave Lucy. You can do this."

A child's shriek sounded, and they both turned to see one of the men carrying

Boone over his shoulder like a mall Santa would a sack of wrapped presents.

"They're coming. Get ready." He motioned at Lucy to back up a few inches, then lowered himself into a squatting position, the tire iron held aloft.

Her heart slammed into her rib cage. How would Noah take out both men without hurting Boone?

THIRTEEN

One of the van doors swung wide, and Noah kicked his legs out as it opened. The door flew right into the blond perp's face, and he howled in pain. The van's location—parked sideways on an incline—aided with the momentum, causing the man to career backward. Noah leaped out and pounced on him, delivering a direct hit to his jaw with the tire iron.

That was all it took. The skinny blond man sprawled unconscious on the cold, hard earth. Noah whipped around, coming face-to-face with the shorter one who'd held Boone. Boone was nowhere in sight now. Good. Noah advanced on the second man quickly so he didn't have time to retrieve any weapons. Too late. The glint of a black pistol caught his eye.

"What'd you do to Donny?" the burly man shouted, raising the weapon and training it on Noah.

Noah dove behind a stump at the same time a feminine cry rent the air. A resounding *whack* followed, like a heavy object slammed into human flesh, then something heavy thudded to the ground.

Noah stumbled upright and cleared the stump to find Lucy brandishing a heavy-duty flashlight, her eyes round with surprise.

"Nice hit." Noah pivoted, searching the tree line. "Where's Boone?"

"I don't know. Hiding, I hope." She gazed at the flashlight. "I'm keeping this."

Noah dragged both men together, then located the wad of rope that had been around Lucy's wrists. He didn't have much length to work with, but he did his best to tie the men's wrists together. A shiny object caught his eye. Cell phone.

Noah snatched the black cell phone from the ground beside the shorter man.

"Boone?" Lucy cupped her hands around her mouth and shouted. "Boone!"

Noah joined her, calling out the child's name.

"Check around the van. I think he went under it." He motioned at the men. "I'm staying here in case they wake up."

She circled the van, then let out a shout. "Found him. You can come out now."

Noah released a huge breath as Lucy coaxed the child from beneath the van. Boone must've scrambled underneath to hide. Thank the Lord he'd stayed nearby.

Noah gripped the cell phone and called 9-1-1. If he wasn't mistaken, they were on the eastern portion of Forest Parkway, not far from Whisper Mountain Tunnel and Jasper's cabin. "I'm calling the police."

Lucy sat on the edge of the van, where the doors were still open. The flashlight lay across her lap. Boone tucked in beside her as Noah spoke to the dispatcher.

He ended the call and joined them. "Authorities are on their way."

"What happens to your friend, the other ranger?"

"They'll arrest him. And I don't know if I'd call Shawn a friend. He was more like an acquaintance. Coworker. No wonder my gut was telling me not to trust him."

Her eyes met his, warm and filled with sympathy. "You saved our lives. More than once." Her mouth tipped up in a soft, appreciative smile.

His throat dried out, and he had to remind himself to breathe. Remind himself that Lucy disliked the woods, that she was probably leaving the area for a new job. That she didn't want the same things he did. Marriage. A family.

"You're so good with kids, Lucy. It seems a shame you don't want any."

She looked away from him, into the woods. "When I said I didn't want kids, it wasn't totally accurate. I do want kids, just not my own."

He cocked his head. "Elaborate."

"My dream is to run a foster home. You know, save up and buy a large, older house. Remodel it, or who am I kidding, have someone else do it. Then I can foster children who were like my brother, Micah, and me. Lost and alone for a time." Her forehead furrowed, and he touched her knee softly.

"That sounds like really important work, Lucy."

"*Necessary* work. I'd love to provide a safe place for kids lost in the shadows of the foster care system."

"It also sounds kind of…lonely."

Her eyes flew to his. "How would it be lonely if children in need are living there with me?"

"You'd be on your own. The only adult, dealing with these kids' difficult emotions, by yourself." He removed his hand from her knee. "That's what I meant by lonely."

The cry of a police siren broke through their intense conversation. She inched away from him.

"Can we finish this later?" he asked.

"I don't think there's much else to say, Noah."

Her soft words felt like bullets piercing his skin.

He stood and shook it off. She was right. They were from two different worlds. Yes, Lucy was beautiful, her kindness and courage admirable, but she clearly didn't have any interest in a long-term relationship or marriage. He'd best drop any ideas about that now.

A Tunnel Creek police cruiser pulled up. Officer Chris Anders jumped out.

"Noah Holt, what did you get yourself wrapped up in now?"

Chris strode over, eyeing the incapacitated van, the two men moaning on the ground, then Lucy and Boone. He whistled.

"This must be Boone Harrington. And his social worker." Anders tipped his chin at Lucy.

"It's them." Noah stood, shook Chris's hand.

"You want to tell me what happened here? The short version?"

Noah recounted what happened the last two hours and the bare bones of the days before that. Anders cuffed the two men, and he and Noah loaded them into the back of the police car. He glanced at Lucy as she spoke to Boone. They'd be giving statements very soon. Right now, he wanted them to have a few minutes to clean up.

"Is there any way you can call in another officer to drop us off at the Whisper Mountain Tunnel ranger station?" The three of them wouldn't fit in Anders's Charger with the two handcuffed perps in the back. "My truck is still parked there. I'll bring them back to the cabin, they can get cleaned up, then come in and give their statements."

"Normally I'd say no, but since there's no room for you three and I know you and your lug of a brother, I can do that." Officer Anders circled the white van one more time, then spoke into his shoulder radio, calling for additional backup.

An hour later Noah steered his blue truck up Jasper's driveway. Thankfully the spare key was still inside the magnetic container near the passenger side front tire. He just hoped Kinsley's SUV was still intact at the Shadow Back Mountain Mine. He'd get it later.

He parked in the garage, then they unloaded from the truck and filed into the cabin. No one spoke, and even Boone was drooping. Poor little guy. He'd been through so much.

Noah surveyed the cabin. Even though they were finally safe, it was hard to let his guard down. He checked all the door and window locks then met Lucy in the upstairs hallway.

"Do you still have the toy animal recorder?" she whispered once Boone was in the bathroom getting cleaned up.

"Yes, it's in my room. Probably best not to bring it up with Boone for now. I don't want to remind him about it then upset him because he can't have it."

She nodded, her eyes flickering to his. "Noah..."

He waited. They hadn't spoken much on the drive back here, and he intended to give her space to deal with the trauma of the last few days.

"I didn't mean to sound cold when we were waiting for the police officer. It's just..."

He held up a hand. "No worries, okay? You and Boone get cleaned up. I'll make something to eat. You'll have to go into the station to give your statements soon."

"What happens after that?"

"They write reports based on your accounts of the last few days. Mine, too. Then they decide what to do with you until the trial. I'd guess the men will plead the Fifth, so who knows how long until the identity of anyone else will be released. You'll both be witnesses, so you'll be put under police protection. At that point we part ways, and you shouldn't have to set foot in the forest again."

"Right. That's good." She stared past him before her gaze flickered into his. "Thank you for always telling me what's going on."

Before he could answer, she turned, knocked on the bathroom door, then slipped inside to help Boone.

Leaving Noah with the stumbling realization that it was going to be very difficult saying goodbye to them.

A half hour later, they finished the cheese pizza he'd heated up then downed root beer floats. Boone burped loudly, and Lucy smiled as Noah matched the sound with his own.

It felt so strange, the sense of relief she felt after their terrifying days in the forest. She stood, gathered their dishes and set them in the sink. Then she addressed

Noah. "Is there any way I can call my supervisor now?"

"Oh, yeah. Here you go." Noah pushed back from the table and rose. He tugged out a small black cell from his pocket. "Jasper texted Chris, the first officer on scene with the white van, and he told me where to find his work cell. This is it." Their fingers brushed when she accepted it, and warmth traveled up her arm.

"Thanks."

She plugged in Melissa's number, then wandered down the hall. The front room was lit by the waning afternoon sunshine and the colorful twinkling Christmas tree.

"Lucy!" Melissa answered. "Where are you? Where is Boone?"

"I'm…" She hesitated. "We're okay. We made it out of the forest. There were men after us, but they were arrested. We're safe now." An unexpected sob caught in her throat. Was this all actually over?

"Is Boone with you?"

"Yes, he's here." She told Melissa the shortened version of the last few days, leaving out how Noah had saved them and protected Boone over and over again. The knot in her throat increased in size until she could barely speak.

"Sounds like you ended up with the right protector. That must've been so scary."

The right protector. "Yeah, for sure. How's Boone's mom doing?"

"She's doing pretty well, actually. Woke up yesterday. Tests are all coming back positive. Her doctors said she could start physical therapy soon, if you can believe that."

"After the last few days, I can believe almost anything."

"So Boone is okay? I'd be glad to keep him if you need to talk to authorities."

"For right now, we both will be going into the station to give our statements. I'm not sure what happens after that." The thought of saying goodbye to Boone— and Noah—caused a pit to open in her middle like the sinkhole in the valley.

A shadow moved across the front window, near the Christmas tree. Lucy gasped and inched backward. "Someone's here." Was the door locked?

"What? Where are you?"

The front door opened, and a large man filled the space. With the setting sun behind him and his face in shadow, the menacing form moved toward her.

"Noah!" Lucy chucked the phone, then snatched a wooden nativity figurine off the coffee table and brandished it. "Who are you?"

Noah pounded down the hallway.

"Lucy, it's Jasper." Noah came up beside her and set a palm on her shoulder. "He's my brother."

Jasper, Noah's brother? She drew in a slow breath and willed her heartbeat to slow. Boone peeked out from behind Noah.

The tall, dark-haired man lowered his outstretched arms and stepped closer. "You good now?"

She nodded, setting the wise man back with the large nativity set.

"You know, if I remember right, Noah

knocked me over the head with that guy when we were kids."

"Did not. I used the cow. And that's no bull."

Jasper groaned, then chuckled, and she watched in muted shock as they bantered back and forth. Jasper set his large bag down beside the stairwell, then enfolded Noah in a brief, hard hug.

"Boy, am I glad to see you." Noah punched Jasper's arm. "Maybe you should knock next time."

"At my own house?"

Boone stared up at the two tall men. Noah pointed. "Boone, this big fella is my brother, Mr. Jasper."

Jasper lowered his hand for a high five. "I heard you were a tough guy."

Boone stuck out his chest. "I am tough."

Lucy sank to the couch as they caught up. She searched for the phone and hit Melissa's number again. It rang twice then went to voice mail. Lucy left a brief message letting her know she was okay.

She rejoined them as they entered the

kitchen, handing Jasper his cell. He was tall and broad like Noah, except with darker hair and eyes, his features rougher and his face more open. Less guarded. Right now, he wore a grin as he leaned against a wall.

"I made some calls. Got an earlier flight home." Jasper glanced from her to Noah. "Remind me of your names?"

"This is Boone Harrington." Noah spoke with emphasis, then met her eyes. "And this is Lucy."

"Lucy Taylor." She stuck out her hand. He enclosed it in his larger one.

Jasper scrutinized her, though she didn't feel threatened. "Jasper Holt."

Jasper turned back to speak with his brother. "I can't believe there are more hidden weapons. Did you know there was a mine shaft that goes that far from the mine?"

"I didn't," Noah murmured. He reached over, tickling Boone when the child trotted back into the room. Jasper changed the subject at the boy's return, explaining that his wife, Kinsley, and his son, Gabe, were staying at Kinsley's friend's house until the case was worked out.

"I'm sorry." She sank down onto a kitchen chair. "You just got back from your honeymoon. Is your wife upset it got cut short?"

Jasper leaned back and linked his hands behind his head. He was older than Noah, and his jovial attitude seemed to soften an outspoken personality. But the concern that shone in his dark eyes, both for his brother's safety and for hers and Boone's, appeared sincere.

"It's part of my job. Kins knows that."

"Still, I wish you didn't have to come back early."

"Far as I can tell, none of this is your— or his—" he motioned at Boone "—fault. Besides, no doubt she'll worm a weekend getaway out of it."

"Oh, man," Noah guffawed. "Bad choice of words about Kinsley."

Lucy looked from one brother to the other. "Why do you say that?"

"Kinsley is a wildlife biologist." Jasper tucked his chin. "I have a feeling we'll end up in a cave or swamp looking for some small animal with way too many legs or no legs at all that my son—our son—will beg her to bring home."

Lucy gave a hesitant smile, shivering a little at the image that brought to mind.

Jasper sobered up. "I need to bring you and Boone into the station this evening. Get your statements." He addressed Noah. "I talked to Chris Anders on my way home. He said both men were pretty incoherent. Get this. When they came to, they told him you ran them off the road and threatened them. Beat them, then tied them up. Regular Rambo, my brother is."

Lucy set her fingertips to her lips. How could they get away with that?

"Right, like that's how it played out." Noah growled under his breath.

"They're criminals. They're protecting their backs." He blinked at Lucy. "Can you two get ready to go? ETD five minutes."

Lucy nodded slowly, her throat suddenly tight. ETD meant estimated time of departure. She glanced at Noah. He wore a brooding expression and didn't meet her eyes.

Was this goodbye, then?

FOURTEEN

Noah stared after Lucy as she and Boone headed down the hallway for the staircase.

Once she started up the stairs, he met Jasper's curious look. "What?"

"You look worried, brother. She'll be in my custody at the station. I'll keep tabs on them." He leaned across the table. "Don't you have a trail to hike in Virginia once you give your statement? You know, your *vacation*?"

Noah twisted sideways to crack his back. He'd likely never see them again once he got back from his hike on the AT. "I'm not sure that's happening this year."

Jasper's brows rose. "What is going on between you two? She didn't take her eyes off you when she was in here. And I've never seen you like this."

"I've never been through anything like this."

"You care about her."

"Yes, I care about her." A lot, but he wouldn't admit that out loud. "We had to survive out there together." He dug a hand through his hair. "It wasn't just me this time. It was the three of us out there. We worked together to keep Boone safe. Keep them both alive." He set his elbows on the table and clasped his hands. "Until Shawn Baxter is caught, I can't relax. So, no hiking on the AT for now."

"I get that." Jasper cocked his head. "There's no doubt this is related to the Harrington-Barnhill case. What troubles me is I was certain we caught the main players. Clearly, we did not." He stood, rinsing his cup in the sink.

Noah rose as well, too antsy to sit.

"I will keep my eyes and ears open and follow due process. They'll be safe at the station." Jasper's work phone buzzed. He tugged it from the counter, his features creasing as he read the screen.

Noah paced the kitchen while he waited for an update. Finally, Jasper ended the call.

"What is it?"

"That was Chief McCoy. He said Judge Avery wants to subpoena Boone and Lucy for testimony for the Harrington case. No surprise there. Once they're questioned, they'll head to Greenville with the FBI. Apparently, they're getting involved." Jasper made a face, then tapped out a text.

"You know as well as I do that once the feds take over, we have no control." Noah flattened his mouth into a straight line. "No say in their safety."

Jasper's eyes lifted from his phone, meeting Noah's. Memories flashed between them. Wrestling matches, basketball practices, hide-and-seek in their house in South Carolina and grieving their dad's death in Cameroon.

"You have to come along tonight to give

your statement… Hold up. Anders is texting."

Noah crossed his arms and counted out the seconds as Jasper frowned at his phone, reading the text from the fellow officer.

"Huh. Weren't you worried about your supervisor? Derek Blanton? Chris said he ran into him. Said Derek has been trying to reach you. I guess he couldn't since your phone is somewhere near…?"

"Dogwood Falls."

At least Derek was okay. Noah uncrossed his arms.

Twenty minutes later, they loaded into Jasper's Charger. Boone and Lucy sat in the back seat, Noah up front with Jasper.

"Everyone okay?" He turned and met her eyes.

Lucy clutched the seat belt across her chest. "I'm ready to get this over with."

Noah nodded, a boulder settling on his chest. He watched the trees fly past as Jasper headed east toward Tunnel Creek and the police station.

Boone chatted with Jasper for a few minutes, clicking one of Gabe's Transformer toys Jasper had given him.

Jasper addressed Lucy. "Noah said you're from Greenville?"

Noah scowled. Leave it to Jasper to make small talk now.

"Yes. We lived there when I was little. My...parents were from that area, too."

Jasper made a snapping sound with his cheek. "Oh. I forgot to mention." He glanced at Noah. "There is a possibility the judge will order you and Boone into WITSEC until this trial is over. That's witness protection."

"Order us? So, there's no other options?"

"WITSEC would keep you safe," Noah said too loudly. He cleared his throat. "I think that's the most important thing at this point." Didn't she remember how close she'd come—they'd all come—to being killed?

"I realize that," she answered. "And I'm willing to do whatever keeps Boone safe."

"What about you?" He felt like a jerk for

being so matter-of-fact about it, but she needed to understand the danger of her situation. "Your safety is important, too."

"I can take care of myself, Noah. I always have."

The hollow sound of her words reminded him of what she'd shared in the woods, days ago. How her dad had left them and then her mom had disappeared as well. Everyone important had let her down, which was why she'd turned out so independent and self-sufficient. Still, this situation didn't allow for that. He fisted his hands. Safety demanded she be cautious. If that meant WITSEC, then she'd have no choice.

"Where are we going?" Boone piped up, breaking the tension in the vehicle.

"To the police station," Jasper answered, sending Noah a cut-it-out look. "You get to talk to a police officer and tell him all about your adventure. And I get to see Dash."

"Dash?" Boone asked.

"He's my K-9 partner. He stayed with

another officer and his family while I was away."

"Do I get to see Mommy soon?"

Noah swiveled to find Lucy wrapping the boy in a side embrace.

"I hope so. I know she wants to see you so much, too." Lucy glanced up, looking past him at Jasper. "My supervisor, Melissa, said she's doing well."

"Thank God for that," Jasper said.

Noah shifted in the seat. Lucy was upset with him. He didn't like it, but it was for the best. Once they gave their statements, she'd remain out of reach, especially if she entered WITSEC and left the area. His stomach dropped. Even if she didn't, he was pretty sure there wasn't a future with her, whether he wanted that or not.

Too late he realized that maybe, just maybe, he did want that.

Jasper guided his police car through the station parking lot. Lucy knotted her hands in her lap as Noah's sharp words replayed in her mind. Didn't he know she would do anything to keep Boone safe? Why had he questioned her like that? Especially now, when they were about to part ways.

She had no idea how this witness protection program worked, but she knew enough to recognize she wouldn't be able to see Noah again. Her throat stung at the thought.

"You want out first, brother?" Jasper slowed near the double front doors.

The Tunnel Creek police station was a wide, one-story brick building with small town written all over it. She'd never been inside, and wished she didn't have to go now. Would Noah give his statement at the same time she and Boone did? She dabbed her knuckle to the corner of her eye as tears threatened.

Why did she care so much what he thought, anyway?

Yes, Noah was dependable, honest. Kind. Not nearly as serious as she'd thought in the beginning, when they first met in the forest. But he loved the outdoors. He was going hiking for his vacation, for goodness' sake. She was happiest around tall buildings and parking lots, with the possibility of a job transfer back to Greenville in her near future. And he wanted a family one day.

There was no doubt he'd be a wonderful dad. Picturing that very thing—Noah with his own child—tweaked her heart, and she blinked hard as more tears threatened.

There was no future with Noah Holt.

He climbed out of the car, then ducked down when Jasper called him back.

"Hold up. Anders is texting again."

Noah nodded, his eyes flickering to Lucy before returning to Jasper.

"They found Kinsley's car up at the mine. He said Derek offered to give you a ride up there so you can bring it back. Get it out of the way before they start the investigation. I've got to stay here, so that would be a big help. That okay?"

"I can do that." Noah's tone was flat. "When I'm finished giving my statement."

He spun to head inside, and Lucy set

a hand on the door handle. What if they never spoke again today…or ever? She didn't even have his cell phone number, yet she knew the ache of loss he'd experienced when he lost his dad. Knew he had a wonderful sense of humor and cared for others deeply. Could she just let him walk away?

She turned to Boone. "I have to talk to Mr. Noah. I'll be right back." Then she touched Jasper's shoulder. "Please, can you stay with him?"

"Take your time," Jasper called as she jumped out and followed Noah to the doors.

"Noah, wait."

A woman exited the building, glancing at them with curiosity.

"Noah?"

When he finally turned, his handsome face was restrained. Polite. The expression he'd worn after he saved them from the river.

"I'm sorry I snapped at you. Don't be mad, please. It's just…" She searched his eyes, looking for the emotional connection they'd had for the last few days. She'd felt it, knew it had existed, even though she hadn't wanted to acknowledge it.

"Noah?" Her heart lifted as his expression softened, and his gaze fell into hers.

Before she could react, he reached out to cup her cheek. "I shouldn't have reacted that way in the car. I'm not mad. Just... please, be careful."

She held still, the warmth of his palm making her chest ache. Then he let go.

"Bye, Lucy. Take care."

"Noah, wait!" She reached into her pocket and pulled out the little stone he'd given her. "Here. I want you to keep it." She handed him the heart-shaped rock before he could say no.

He looked down at the stone for several seconds, then closed his hand around it and spun away from her. The bitter wind toyed with her hair as he strode into the station.

Noah was gone. She'd never felt so alone, even when her parents left her and

Micah by themselves at the campsite when she was a child.

Jasper strolled up, Boone riding piggy-back on him. Just like he had on Noah.

He stopped beside her. "You okay?"

"I guess not." Lucy sniffled, and was embarrassed when tears spilled out. She wiped her nose. "He doesn't want anything to do with me."

"I don't think that's true." Jasper set Boone down.

"He just walked away." She hiccupped on a sob, and Jasper reached out to pat her arm.

"You know, my brother had a girlfriend when he was in college. They almost got engaged. Tessa. She ended up moving to DC instead. She was into all that political stuff. Campaigns. Whatever. He barely spoke about it, but if I remember right, she loved Noah's mission in life more than she loved...him. That situation made him guarded."

"How could she leave him for politics?"

"You got me. Her loss, right?"

"Yes." And what a loss. There weren't many men like Noah. "It doesn't help that I made it clear I have no interest in marriage. Plus, I'm not an outdoorsy-type person at all."

"Hey, my wife loves bugs. I hate them. She picks up snakes. *On purpose*, mind you. I'd prefer all snakes are sent to Antarctica for an extended trip." He winked at her. "But, I can't live without Kins. So there is that."

Lucy smiled despite her heavy emotions.

Jasper continued. "If you do care, you should tell him how you feel."

"He just told me goodbye like he doesn't want anything to do with me. I can't blame him, after all the problems I've brought into his life."

"None of which are your fault." He swung Boone's arm playfully, then tickled the child, who squealed and dodged away. "When my wife—man, it sounds so cool saying that. Anyway, when Kinsley, my wife, came back to Tunnel Creek, she ended up being the target of some dangerous people."

"The ones who were arrested at the Whisper Mountain Tunnel?"

"Yes. Them." His features tightened, and she glimpsed the protective side of Jasper Holt. "We stumbled on some guns stashed in the tunnel after she came back to town for her aunt's memorial service. Turned out her aunt found some dirt on the gun smugglers and was killed because of it. Then they came after Kinsley. She believed she brought trouble into my life, too. So she kept herself apart from me, you know? I guess I did, too." He made a thinking sound. "Anyway, yeah, the situation was dangerous, but I cared about her and wanted to protect her. That's what Noah was doing for you, too."

"Exactly. He's doing his job."

He shook his head. "I'm pretty certain it's more than that to him now. Way more."

It was her turn to shake her head. Noah might care about her, but he didn't want to get involved. She still wasn't sure what she wanted in her future. Marriage had never been a possibility or a desire on her part. But with Noah...

Jasper watched her like he could read her thoughts and emotions. "If you don't care, then that's it, you know? There's nothing more to say. But if you do care, at least tell him."

"I care too much, which is why I want to protect him."

"Noah needs protection like my K-9 partner, Dash, needs another squeaky toy."

She covered her face with her hands. "Have you ever made a personal decision because you wanted to protect yourself, only later, you realized the decision isn't actually best for you?"

"Probably. Maybe it's as simple as you made the best decision for yourself at the time, then things changed. A door opened that you feel safe to walk through."

She dropped her hands and gaped at him. Could that be true for her?

"C'mon. Let's get you two inside. Noah's giving his statement, then it's your turn. There's coffee, drinks and snacks in the lobby if you want anything."

She followed Jasper inside but couldn't deny she'd rather be following Noah.

Noah loaded into Derek's old Expedition, then they headed west into Sumter. He cradled the gray heart-shaped stone he'd given Lucy in his palm. Why had she given it back to him?

The sun was setting, and winter's cold fingers snuck into the truck. Holiday music filtered through the interior of the vehicle. Christmas was only a couple of weeks away, but instead of joy, a sense of gloom weighed down Noah's limbs.

Jasper had been waiting for him after Noah finished giving his statement. There'd been no sign of Lucy and Boone. Before Noah left with Derek, Jasper mentioned there was an APB out for Shawn Baxter. Lord willing, the younger man was located and arrested.

Noah filled his cheeks up with air, then blew it out. What a waste of a good life.

"I heard they caught some men involved with the gun smuggling up at Shadow Back Mountain Mine. It's crazy that people were hiding stuff up there."

"Yeah, it was a shock for sure." Noah ran his thumb over the little stone. "It's disappointing discovering all this crime in Tunnel Creek and Sumter."

"Agreed. Now they just need to get Shawn." Derek shook his head. "I can't believe I didn't see that one coming."

"None of us did." Except he *had* experienced a sense of reserve about Shawn from the get-go. But Derek had hired him, so Noah wouldn't mention it. He didn't want to accuse his boss of bad judgment.

"Oh, hey, I'm sorry about being MIA. I had some family stuff to deal with near Greenville."

"Everything okay?" Noah placed the little stone in a shallow tray in the passenger door and glanced at Derek.

"Yeah, just trying to figure out how to help my sister make ends meet around the holidays. You know, people need money.

Same old, same old." Derek turned the radio down. "So, what happened out there? I heard they finally got the social worker's car out of the river. Was there something these men were looking for? Evidence?"

"It was a voice recording toy that Boone's mom used to record her husband's murderers." He squeezed the back of his neck. "I don't really want to talk about all that right now."

"Hey, I get that."

As the truck neared the copper mine, Noah's mind reversed to the last couple hours. He'd given his statement as quickly as possible, then met Derek out front. Lucy and Boone were up at bat now. How would Boone do, recalling all the events they experienced together? And Lucy?

His jaw tightened. It would be hard on them. He'd considered staying, but it was better this way. A clean break. He'd ask Jasper about them later. If at all.

"Noah. Did you hear me?" Derek lightly punched Noah's left arm.

"What? Sorry, I wasn't paying attention."

"I said do you have the keys to your sister-in-law's car?"

He set the back of his skull against the headrest. "I hid them beneath the ticket booth."

"Ah, I get it. You were in James Bond mode."

"More like I was in trying-to-keep-Lucy-and-Boone-alive mode." The words felt sharp on his tongue. "Sorry. I'm just strung tight about all this."

"Not a problem, man. I get it. You still planning on hiking the AT after all this? Might be relaxing for you to get away."

Noah shrugged. "I might wait until the spring."

"Change of plans, huh?" Derek glanced at him. "Wait a minute, do you have a thing for that pretty social worker?"

"Her name is Lucy. And nah," he lied. "I just think it's better to stick around here. Help out Jasper with the investigation in any way I can."

"Gotcha." Derek pulled into the Shadow Back Mountain Mine lot. "We're here."

The sun was setting over the mountain peak, sending waves of gold and pink across the horizon. *God's unique color palette*, his mom always said. But the beauty that normally invigorated him created an ache of loneliness in his chest.

Lucy. He should've told her how he felt. Problem was, he couldn't quite pin down his feelings for Lucy. *Complicated*, that was for sure.

"You look like a lost puppy."

Noah glared at Derek.

Derek parked, then put his hands in the air in an expression of innocence.

They both exited the Expedition and shut the doors. Noah circled the back of the SUV, then set the edge of his palm to his forehead and looked out over Shadow Back Mountain and the little town that had almost been his demise. A cold wind whistled across the valley, and the small structures that made up the town appeared miniature in the distance.

"I heard you fell down into a sinkhole? That had to be rough."

"Yep. Very dark, lots of dirt. Claustrophobic." He shuddered. "I'm just glad it was me down there and not her."

Derek guffawed. "Wow, man. You've got it bad."

Noah dropped his hand from his brow but didn't deny anything. What was the point?

"Should you find the keys before I head out?"

"I'm good. Thanks for the ride." Noah walked toward the ticket booth.

"Enjoy your time off," Derek called.

Yeah, right. Noah gave a wave as his boss climbed back in his Expedition. Then he crouched, digging in the ground beneath the bushes, locating Kinsley's silver key chain and her fob. When he stood, his head started pounding.

He turned to Kinsley's car and lifted the car remote, then froze. *The heart-shaped stone.* He'd left it in Derek's vehicle. Why it mattered so much to him, he didn't understand. He just knew that it did.

Noah turned, jogging across the parking lot to Derek's Expedition. His friend had backed up, and Noah caught him right when the white reverse lights were turned off.

"Hey, Derek. Wait!"

Derek glanced his way, wearing a strange expression. Frustration and impatience. Then anger. Noah slowed as he approached the Expedition.

"I left something in the doorframe. Can I..." He paused as Derek's mouth turned down. Had something else happened? "Do you mind if I grab it?"

"Yeah, hurry up. I have someplace to be."

Where had Derek's dark mood come from? Noah circled the large truck, frowning. Noah tried the door but it was locked. "Hold on," Derek mouthed. He started rolling the window down, and Noah stretched an arm inside, grabbing the stone.

"Got it. Thanks." Then he stepped away and clicked Kinsley's fob.

An enormous explosion filled Noah's peripheral vision. The blast knocked him back into the Expedition. A volcano of volatile black and red flames leaped into the sky, and a pulsing wave of heat carried over. Noah dove to the ground as fire swallowed Kinsley's car.

A bomb? Someone had rigged a bomb inside the vehicle.

The Expedition's tires squealed on the gravel, and an electric current jolted Noah's blood. Derek? He was part of this?

Noah jumped to his feet and raced up behind the moving car. The tires squealed again as Derek tried to drive away. Noah reached through the open window, landing a quick, hard jab to Derek's jaw. The car slowed, and Derek's head bounced into the headrest.

"Get off me!"

Noah unlocked the vehicle through the window and tugged open the door. "*You* are involved in this?" Shock added to his strength. He unlatched Derek's seat belt and yanked him outside the car.

"Don't touch me!" Derek kicked at him as Noah punched his face. Then Noah kneeled on his chest and arms, fisting Derek's collar.

"Why did you do this? Were you trying to kill me?"

Derek sneered at him. "You can't prove anything."

"Why would you do this?" Shawn *and* Derek? Noah's pulse pounded in his temples.

"You and your brother. Always getting in the way. Barnhill wanted Dean Hammond to invite Jasper into the group, and Hammond knew he'd say no. Just like I knew you would."

"Barnhill got you involved in this? Wait, did you have him killed before he could rat you out?"

Derek closed his bruised red eyes. "I'm not telling you anything."

"Smuggling those weapons leads to increased crime in cities. People die because of them."

"Do I look like I care?" Derek snarled.

"Of course you don't." A sour taste filled Noah's mouth. "What would Emma think of this? Please tell me she's not part of it, too?"

"Emma and I broke up this summer, remember? I met someone new, someone who isn't afraid to take risks sometimes if it means gain. *Financial* gain." Derek sneered. "Her name is Melissa."

"Risks as in, illegal activity?" Déjà vu pinged Noah's brain. *Melissa? That name...* "Wait a minute. Lucy's supervisor is named Melissa."

Derek lunged upward, bringing a knee into Noah's back. It knocked the wind out of him, and then Derek shoved him off and rolled away. Noah jumped up and flew after him, dragging Derek back to the ground and throwing another punch. Blood spurted from Derek's nose, and he howled in pain.

"You knock me out and you'll never find

out where your girlfriend and that kid are going."

Noah froze. "What are you doing with them?" Weren't they going to Greenville with an FBI agent?

"They're on their way to a similar fate. Except not with a bomb." He laughed, and more blood trickled from his nose. "We took out an FBI agent and replaced him with one of our men."

Noah laid one more solid hit to Derek's face. The man's head jerked back, then he passed out. Noah grabbed Derek's cell phone and jumped into the Expedition. He jammed it into Drive and sped from the parking lot. He had to get to her in time.

FIFTEEN

"Where're we going now?" Boone wiggled his hand in Lucy's as they walked out of the Tunnel Creek police station with Jasper. Dash, Jasper's handsome K-9 partner, trotted beside them. Boone had lost his mind about the brindle-colored dog, asking to walk him and pet him and if he could keep him.

She let out a weary sigh.

Jasper had secured Boone's toy dog, and it was on route to a lab for voice-analyzing. She and Boone had given their statements, spoken at length to Chief McCoy, split a bagel that served as dinner and now they were headed to Greenville. They'd spend the night in a hotel and meet with the attorneys and judge tomorrow. Lucy had also called Margie, her neighbor, to ask her to feed her betta fish and check her mail.

"I love Dash." Boone stroked the dog's back, and Dash gave his cheek a quick lick.

"He's a good boy," Jasper commented. "No tongue, Dash. My son, Gabe, likes to nap with him."

"I don't like naps."

"Neither does Gabe. Dash makes a great pillow, though."

Lucy pressed her lips together. Boone would end up with his maternal aunt and uncle until his mom was well enough to care for him again. His life was forever altered, but he would be safe and stay with his immediate family. *Thank You for that, Lord.*

Twilight slipped over the town, streaking the horizon with gold and pink swaths of color. Her breath caught. Had she noticed this kind of beauty before being stuck in the forest with Noah? No, not really. His love of God's creation must've rubbed off on her.

Jasper's cell chimed, and he pulled it from his pocket. Dash sat immediately at his master's side, which meant Boone stayed right there, too.

"Holt here." A series of *hmm*s and *huh*s followed, then he agreed to something and ended the call. "Sounds like officers found Shawn Baxter in an abandoned house on the outskirts of town. It's a standoff. I'm needed there ASAP." He peered at a dark sedan parked in a visitor spot in the parking lot. "Looks like the FBI agent is here."

A dark-haired man in black slacks and a blue polo exited the sedan's driver's side door. The man's gaze bounced off Jasper, his eyes widening when he noticed Dash.

The dog whined, stood up and danced in a circle, then sat again.

"Dash. Heel."

The man edged away from the imposing police dog as he approached them. He looked directly at her. "You must be Lucy Taylor. And this is Boone?"

Boone shrunk away from the man, hiding behind Dash.

"Yes. I'm sorry, he's had a rough couple of days," Lucy explained. "And you are...?"

"Agent Rick Denson. I'll be taking you to Greenville tonight so you can see the judge tomorrow."

She nodded, trying to catch Jasper's eye. He was speaking to an officer who'd pulled up behind the FBI agent. Finally, he turned to the FBI agent.

"I'm Officer Jasper Holt, Tunnel Creek PD."

"Agent Denson." Rick flashed a shiny badge, then tucked it back in his pocket. "I'd like to get going. There's paperwork the judge gave me that needs filled out before tomorrow."

"Then I'll let you take it from here." Jasper addressed Lucy as the FBI agent walked around his car and slid inside. "I'm only a call away if you need anything. And, Lucy, don't forget what I said earlier."

"I won't. Thank you so much, Jasper." Her chin sank to her chest. Jasper had given her Noah's cell number, then reminded her Noah would have to get a new phone since his had been lost in the woods. She watched Jasper and Dash climb into his police car. The lights flipped on. Once he hit the main road, his sirens blared.

God, please watch over Jasper.

"That was an intimidating dog," the FBI agent commented from the driver's seat.

She gave a weak nod. All she could think of was that she was leaving. Heading to Greenville and an unknown future. Was it only a week ago she'd entertained the idea of moving back there for a job? Now Greenville felt like a million miles away from Tunnel Creek.

Lucy opened the back passenger door for Boone, then climbed in after him.

She buckled her seat belt and his, her thoughts returning to Noah. Jasper mentioned that Noah had gone to retrieve Kinsley's car from the mine parking lot. An ache formed in her chest. Was it hard for him to go back there after what happened with the sinkhole? And the little heart-shaped stone... Why hadn't she kept it?

"I got snacks." Agent Denson tossed back two packages of Twinkies. Lucy wrinkled her nose at the same time Boone exclaimed his excitement.

Lucy held one of the sugary snacks. "Why don't we split this." After she handed him his half, she pulled the bottled water Jasper had given her out of her purse. Boone shoved the entire half of the Twinkie in his mouth.

Commence sugar high in three, two, one...

"That was yummy."

A dot of white cream hid in the crease of his lower lip, and she wiped it off gently with her thumb. Boone grinned. It felt odd smiling after all they'd been through this week, but the gesture was genuine. How sweet and strong this young boy was.

"Do you happen to have any wipes or napkins in this—"

"Nope," Agent Denson cut her off.

She retrieved the burner phone Jasper gave her in the station. "Are we going straight to Greenville?"

"Yep."

He wasn't the chatty type, which worked for her. They drove for several minutes, cutting through the main streets in town. Then the agent's phone rang. It must've been tied into the car's system, because the radio's voice spoke out loud. "Incoming call from Black Bird." Agent Denson punched a button, and the voice stopped even though the phone continued ringing. He muttered irritably to himself.

Lucy's pulse took off in a sprint. *Black Bird?* Wasn't that the nickname for Shawn Baxter, the other ranger? She must've heard wrong. Why would this agent have his CB radio code name on his phone?

"Would you mind taking a quick detour? I need to—"

"No time for that, Ms. Turner. Not tonight."

Taylor, she almost corrected him. *Not tonight?* What did that mean?

He glanced at her in the rearview mirror, then his gaze dropped. Could he see that she was holding the phone?

The car sped up as they entered the tree line. It was dark now, and he was driving fast. Too fast. They were leaving Tunnel Creek behind and entering Sumter on their way to Greenville. But the fear she'd once felt in the woods was gone. This was Noah's world, and he'd let her into it without even realizing it. He loved these trees, these rocks, and the streams and rivers that made up the forest. And his love had helped her overcome her fear and anxiety that being in the woods used to cause.

Please, Lord, help us get away from this man.

"Ugh, that Twinkie was old. I feel sick to my stomach." She made a nauseated sound. "I need you to pull over."

"In the woods? Not happening, lady." He didn't even bother looking at her. Did he know she recognized the man's call name? No, he wouldn't. She had to play it cool. Remain calm. Boone stared at her as she dialed 9-1-1, her fingers trembling so hard it was difficult pressing buttons.

"Please, I'm going to be sick," she tried again, nearly shouting. "Do you want me throwing up in your car, Agent Denson? Right here on Forest Parkway?" She spoke loudly to cover the 9-1-1 dispatcher who'd no doubt answered and was listening to them.

"Why're you talking like that?" His eyes narrowed at her through the mirror. "No, we're not stopping."

She leaned forward, her forehead almost to the driver's headrest, setting her hand on her mouth in case the man shot another glance in the rearview mirror. Then she made a gruesome noise, pressing her other hand to her middle. The faint sound of a woman's voice on the other end of the line confirmed the dispatcher had answered and could hear them.

"Ms. Lucy?" Boone shrunk away from her. "Oh no, oh no, are you gonna throw up?"

The driver muttered an oath, then swerved

to the side of the road. If only she could put her phone on speaker. She prayed that the woman on the other end of the call would hear some of their conversation, trace her phone and send help right away.

Please, Lord...

The driver—was his name even Denson?—jumped out and opened her door. The car was still partially parked on the road. His movements were sharp and jerky as he stepped back. "You have one minute to empty your stomach over there." He pointed to the brown foliage and rising hill just past the roadside.

"Ugh. I'm coming." Lucy shivered from real fear and the cool air filling the interior of the car. She edged closer to Boone, reaching across to raise the door lock. It didn't budge. The driver must've engaged the child locks. She flicked her eyes at the child, who was squishing the other wrapped Twinkie between his palms.

"Listen to me, Boone. When I go around the car, jump out my door and run. But make sure there aren't any cars coming."

He stared at her with those big brown eyes, his mouth trembling.

"You can do it. *Run*."

She stepped out and pretended to stumble, bent over and moaning. She had nothing to hit or attack him with other than her phone and the element of surprise. And Boone was stuck inside. Rounding the back of the car, she bumped her hip into it like she felt sick and could barely walk. Which also was partly true. Adrenaline pumped through her system so fast her muscles quaked and her bones felt rubbery.

The man followed her, throwing his arms out in agitation. "Get off the road. I don't have time for this." His caring-but-rushed-FBI-agent veneer had broken apart, revealing an angry man in need of manners. "We have to rendezvous in thirty minutes."

Where she was certain they'd be meeting the man behind all this. The *Big Man*? The one who likely had control over the huge stash of illegal weapons in the mine tunnels at Shadow Back Mountain. She squeezed the cell phone. Had the dispatcher sent help yet?

Lucy edged toward the side of the car. If only she could open Boone's door. She would never be able to forgive herself if Boone was stolen from her now.

She let out another grotesque noise, then pretended to fall against the car, knocking into Boone's window. He looked up at her from inside, and she waggled her brows. Would he get the hint and jump out?

She chanced a glance at the man. His cold, hard eyes clashed into hers, then narrowed. "What're you doing? I thought you were gonna be sick?"

He was onto her. It was now or never. She groaned. "I am. Watch out." She fell toward him, throwing her left arm out and slapping the cell phone into his head.

"Hey, what are you doing?" He shoved her back, onto the concrete. Pain jarred her elbows as she landed hard. From her sprawled position, she noticed two small feet appear on the other side of the car, then take off. Thank the Lord, Boone had gotten away.

The roar of a car engine filled her ears. Someone was driving right toward her.

She screamed, curling into a ball on the road.

The large SUV's brakes squealed so close she smelled the burnt rubber. When she opened her eyes, the hulking vehicle nearly straddled her. Not a police car. Lucy clenched her eyes shut. She didn't stand a chance now. At least Boone had gotten away. Hopefully far enough.

The fake FBI agent ignored her, staring up at the SUV instead. "Great. Now the Big Man will know you tricked me. Hey, Derek, I was trying to— What in the—"

Lucy gasped as Noah leaped from the truck and tore toward their kidnapper. They fell in a grunting heap near her. She clambered upright, but not before the man's arm snaked around her, grabbing her against himself as he leaped to his feet.

"Back up," Denson—or whatever his

name was—shouted in her ear. Blood trickled from his nose. "Get away or something bad happens to her."

"Let her go." Noah's voice was low, angrier than she'd ever heard it, and his gaze was pinned to her captor's face. "Lucy. I'm here."

"Noah." Saying his name and seeing him in person again calmed her galloping heart.

"Are you hurt?" He edged in closer, his hands up.

"Step back!" The man's arm moved up around her neck. He squeezed until stars dotted her vision.

"Noah," she pleaded.

"Hey, man," Noah muttered, placating. "Okay. I stopped. Let's just talk this out." Noah wore that determined expression she'd come to recognize. He was fighting for her, like he had the last few days.

She met his eyes under the truck's headlights. His flicked to the ground. Then again. The man's feet? He was telling her what to do.

Lucy lifted her right foot and slammed her heel down onto the man's toe. He let out a pained cry and loosened his hold just enough so she could scramble away. She clambered around the front of the car as Noah and the man fought.

Sirens rang out in the distance, growing louder. "Noah. The police are coming."

Noah's arm wrapped around the man's throat from behind.

"Let go of me." The fake agent's words were strangled.

"Not happening."

An unmarked police car pulled in behind the SUV, lights flashing. Jasper? He and his K-9 partner exploded from the vehicle. Dash was at Noah's side in an instant, and his ferocious bark sounded like repeated explosions. Noah released the driver. He climbed onto the roof of the car, shrieking as Dash leaped at him, teeth bared.

Jasper shouted a command, and the dog sank to his haunches in front of the cowering criminal, his tongue out and his alert gaze never wavering.

Behind them, two more police cars swerved into the area and parked. More officers joined the scene, guns drawn.

Jasper rushed forward and handcuffed the man, then spoke to Noah. "Shawn Baxter has been arrested. He sustained a gunshot wound but looks like he'll survive to spend time behind bars. Officer Anders arrived at the mine minutes ago. He cuffed Derek Blanton and he's bringing him in."

"Good." Noah scrubbed his hand down his face. His poor eye was already turning black-and-blue.

Where was Boone? She glanced around then called his name. He popped out from the tree line, then scurried over to her. Noah treaded over to them as she hugged the child.

"Mr. Noah saved us. And Dash did, too."

"Yes, he did. Again." She tucked Boone in front of herself.

Noah moved closer, wiping a trickle of blood beneath his nose. "I think this is finally over."

Did he mean that? She cupped a hand over her mouth and muffled a sob.

Boone tipped his head to look up at her. "Are you sad, Ms. Lucy?"

"No, not sad. These are happy tears."

"Can I have another Twinkie?" Boone tugged her hand.

She smiled. "Not right now. You've had enough sugar."

"It makes me run super fast."

"You did run super fast. That's true."

Jasper shoved the FBI imposter in the back of his car and shut the door, then addressed the other officers. They were gathered into a circle, discussing the events of the evening. Boone darted over to pet the dog, who licked the boy's cheek.

"Dash, no tongue," Jasper warned.

"He can lick me! He can lick me!" Boone stroked the dog's brindle fur.

Lucy and Noah shared a smile.

He stepped closer. "Are you okay?"

"I am now." She rubbed her arms vigorously. Her elbow still stung from the fall earlier. "I'm always okay when you're with me."

Jasper strode over to them.

"I'm taking this guy into the station. Boone can come with us. I'm afraid we'll need another statement from both of you."

She nodded, then turned to Noah. Words fled as she gazed at the man who had saved her life and taught her to trust others—and God—in the process.

Noah ran a hand over his hair, flicking out a twig and some pebbles from the scuffle. He had so much to say to her, but the words scattered like the gravel when he'd fought her kidnapper. Lucy leaned in to help clean him up, and he was glad she couldn't hear his sprinting heartbeat or read his mind.

"I'm so disappointed Melissa is involved with this. She didn't seem capable of something so awful."

"I feel the same about Derek."

He didn't want to talk about the people who had betrayed them. Instead, he longed to share how he felt. How she made him feel. He couldn't take his eyes off her. She was so beautiful and strong, his Lucy. Even with her long dark hair a mess and dirt smudges on her cheek.

"Thank you for saving me. Saving us. Again."

He shook his head. "*You* actually saved *me* this time."

"I did not."

"You did. Look." Noah withdrew the small gray heart-shaped rock from his pocket. "See this? When you gave this back to me, I held on to it. But then I left it in Derek's car when we drove to the mine. He, uh, he had rigged up Kinsley's car with a bomb when the lock was disarmed, but at the last moment I remembered I'd left this stone in his truck. I ran back over and got it. That's when I clicked to unlock her car and it exploded."

She covered her mouth and moaned his

name from between her fingers. "You almost... You would've died."

"But I didn't. Because of this little rock. So, I'd say we're even." He reached over, lifting a stray lock of hair that had caught on her lips, tucking it behind her ear.

"Noah." She peered up at him, her eyes softer than he'd ever seen them. Then she threw her arms around him. He lifted her against his chest and held tight. A low, contented sigh came from deep inside him. How right this felt.

When they separated, he didn't think. He just spoke. "What if I don't want you to leave me again?"

His words hung in the air, a question, a statement and their future all wrapped up in one.

"Noah...?"

"Just listen. I respect you and your choices about your future. I know what happened to you, and how it affected your life and decisions. When we were younger, my mom told us kids that one day we'd meet someone we could laugh and cry with and all the in-between. That's how we'd know without a doubt they were the right person for us. And the thing is, Lucy, I want that with you. Laughter and tears, but mostly laughter. And all the in-between. Because the moments I've spent with you have been the best moments of my life."

A tear spilled down her cheek. He used the pad of his thumb to gently wipe it away, then cupped her face. "Even though we were almost killed?"

"Well, except for that part," he chuckled.

"Mine, too. The best moments of my life," she whispered. "And..."

"And...?" he prompted quietly, all the oxygen in Tunnel Creek stopped up in his chest.

"I don't ever want to leave you again."

"You don't?" He grinned like a fool. A fool in love. "This is convenient. Very convenient." Then he sobered up. "We don't have to rush anything. We can learn to love each other first, then figure out the next steps."

"I've never wanted anything more, Noah."

"You're sure?"

"Yes."

He stilled, holding her gaze intently, then leaned in to brush a kiss to her forehead.

She stood on her tiptoes and brought her lips to his in a kiss that made him forget they needed to head back to the station to give their statements.

When they pulled apart, a wide smile spread across her beautiful face. "This *is* very convenient."

"And God is good." He clasped her hands and led her toward the vehicle and their future.

"And God is *very* good."

EPILOGUE

"**W**here exactly are you taking me?" Lucy asked Noah as he guided her to the top of Dogwood Falls. It had been eleven months since the fateful night she was forced off the road and her car ended up in the Broken Branch River. This was her first time back in the area.

"It's a surprise."

Her fear of the woods had evolved into an enjoyment of God's creation. Not to mention the pleasure of alone time, hiking through the forest, just her and Noah. But for some reason, on this crisp, sunny fall day, he wasn't telling her exactly where they were going.

"Look at that." Noah slowed, pointing

at the cascade of falling water glimmering on the rocks beside them.

"What is it?" She adjusted her pack, a purple-and-green mesh bag he'd given her for her birthday in May.

"See the colors? That's a river rainbow. When the sun hits the mist coming off the water just right, there's a rainbow."

Sure enough, a small colorful spot hovered over the upper section of the waterfall, glinting like a jewel in the crisp air. "Oh, I do. It's so pretty."

"Come on, let's get up there and find a spot to eat. I'm starving."

He'd packed sandwiches, apples and drinks earlier. Said this was a special outing. She assumed it was about the promotion he'd received at work. Noah had taken Derek's position as supervisor of the northwest quadrant. "You're always hungry."

"Nothing wrong with that."

"Can I have your metabolism?"

He ushered her up the last section of the

waterfall. "You're beautiful just the way you are."

Warmth climbed her neck despite the cool fall temperatures. Noah liked to throw out random compliments that were both sincere and sweet. And sometimes teasing. She'd gotten used to the teasing, especially since Jasper and their mom, Dana, all meant it from a place of love. Even Brielle joined in on the banter.

So much had happened since Noah subdued Derek and the fake FBI agent that night last December. Once the Shadow Back Mountain Mine gun cache was discovered, the FBI took over the investigation. The real FBI, not Agent Denson—who was actually named Alex Daniels. Alex, Shawn Baxter and Derek Blanton were in prison for a variety of charges, spending at least the next twenty-five years there, along with Nick and Donny. Donny had shortened his sentence by admitting they paid a prison worker to inject David Barnhill with a medicine that killed him, to keep the former mayor quiet.

Her supervisor, Melissa, was also spending the next five years in a women's correctional facility for her part in the illegal operation. Melissa had sent Boone with Lucy on purpose at Derek's bidding.

But God had kept them safe, with Noah's help.

Lucy had taken a leave of absence from social work. She'd passed on the job in Greenville, and she still visited Boone periodically to help out Mrs. Harrington, who'd left the hospital a few weeks after her husband's murder. At Noah's urging, she'd contacted her mom and dad. It would be a long process, but she realized he was right. Forgiveness was necessary to heal. Lucy also watched Gabe when Kinsley and Jasper were working and Dana Holt was teaching her art classes.

Noah had purchased a house on the edge of Sumter National Forest from Elsa Tuttle, an older widow who was friends with the family. Not far from Jasper's cabin.

He'd be moving in once Elsa was settled in her condo in town. Soon.

All in all, life was busy but full.

"So, what are we doing out here? Reliving old memories?" she teased.

"I just wanted you to myself." He roped an arm around her waist and pulled her into a quick hug. "You're sure you don't mind being back here?"

"Not if I'm with you."

He kissed her forehead, then they set off toward the river. Noah ushered her into a wide, fern-filled meadow that hugged the sides of the Broken Branch River. She ambled through the ferns, touching their tops with her fingers. A year ago, they were running for their lives. Now, birdsong and the wind whispered peacefully to them.

"Did you talk to Kinsley?" Noah asked. "How's she feeling?"

They'd gotten the exciting news that Kinsley and Jasper were expecting their first child the other day. Kinsley had become a close friend in the months since Lucy met Noah.

"Poor thing. She's surviving on oranges, peanut butter and Sprite."

"That's an unusual menu."

"Pregnancy cravings." Her smile faltered.

It was out here in these woods that she'd told Noah she didn't want kids. Now she realized she hadn't met the person she could picture herself having a family with. Someone she trusted completely. But with Noah, that had all changed. She still longed to establish a safe house for foster children one day, and Noah had promised they'd do that if and when the opportunity presented itself. But for now, she basked in his loyalty, trusted his heart and knew he would put her—and any future children—first.

"Here we go." Noah took off his pack and unzipped it. He dug out a dark blue paint-flecked quilt and laid it in a clearing a few feet from the river. The steady *whoosh* of the water was background music as they settled on top of it, munching on the sandwiches and discussing Thanksgiving plans. Then they lay on their backs, side by side with hands linked, gazing through the trees at the bright blue sky.

"You were right, Noah."

"That's never a bad thing to hear."

She gave his hand a squeeze. "You were right about God's creation. It is peaceful out here. I would still be scared of all this if it weren't for you." A lump formed in her throat. "And I would still be alone if not for you."

"Lucy."

Noah's voice had changed, and she turned her head to look at him.

He sat up and blew out an unsteady breath. "I know things started out…rough with us. But having you in my life is more than I could've imagined. I still can't believe God blessed me with you."

She slowly rose to a sitting position. "What about when I'm talkative and I ask you too many questions?"

"Even then." He swallowed. "You taught me to communicate more, to rely on others, and that's a good thing. That's part of what I love about you. Also, your kindness and courage, and your sense of humor. How you care for others inspires me. Boone wouldn't have survived without you last year."

"You're the one who kept us alive."

"I helped. We worked together. But *you* kept him alive. You're stronger than you think. My brave Lucy."

Her heart expanded until it felt like it would burst. "I love you, Noah."

His mouth quirked as he reached into his backpack. "Do you…love me enough to eat one more piece of beef jerky?"

She giggled. "Please tell me you did not bring those little meat sticks along. I don't think— Noah?"

He was kneeling now, and in his hand, he held a single stick of beef jerky.

"What is…" A sparkling diamond snatched her attention. A ring? It was caught on the snack food like a mini ring toss. She pressed her folded hands to her mouth. "Noah? Is that…?"

"Lucy Brooke Taylor, will you make me the most blessed man alive and marry me?"

She flung herself at him, wrapping her arms around his neck. "Yes." She kissed him. "Of course. Just please don't make me eat that again."

He let out a loud crack of laughter, then slipped the ring onto her finger. "I wouldn't dare."

"I can't believe you did this. Planned it all. Oh, this ring. Noah. It's so beautiful." Tears filled her eyes as she dropped her gaze to the stunning symbol of his love and loyalty.

Then Noah drew her close and kissed her while the sun shone on their promise of forever.

* * * * *

*If you liked this story from
Kerry Johnson, check out her previous
Love Inspired Suspense books,*

Snowstorm Sabotage
Tunnel Creek Ambush

*Available now from
Love Inspired Suspense!*

*Find more great reads at
www.LoveInspired.com.*

Dear Reader,

I'm thrilled to have you join Lucy, Noah and Boone on their dangerous adventure. For Lucy, getting chased through Sumter National Forest brings back traumatic childhood memories. In fact, that trauma is a large reason why she struggles with abandonment issues and believes that God doesn't care about her.

Lucy had to let go of those past hurts in order to trust Noah and trust God again. The Bible reminds us God is trustworthy and faithful. Jesus is the same yesterday, today and forever. He is a strong tower, our refuge and strength, and an ever-present help in times of trouble. What comforting truths that I hope you cling to today.

I love connecting with readers! Look for me on Facebook (Kerry Johnson Author), Instagram or on my website, www. kerryjohnsonbooks.com, where you can sign up for my quarterly newsletter. God bless you and keep you.

Fondly,
Kerry Johnson